Richard Chandler, England) Society of Dilettanti (London

Antiquities of Ionia

Richard Chandler, England) Society of Dilettanti (London

Antiquities of Ionia

ISBN/EAN: 9783742844996

Manufactured in Europe, USA, Canada, Australia, Japa

Cover: Foto ©Andreas Hilbeck / pixelio.de

Manufactured and distributed by brebook publishing software
(www.brebook.com)

Richard Chandler, England) Society of Dilettanti (London

Antiquities of Ionia

ANTIQUITIES

OF

IONIA.

PUBLISHED BY THE SOCIETY

OF

DILETTANTI.

PART THE FOURTH.

LONDON :

MACMILLAN AND Co.,

29 AND 30, BEDFORD STREET, COVENT GARDEN, W.C.

1881.

PUBLICATIONS OF THE SOCIETY OF DILETTANTI.

PREFACE.

ABOUT the middle of the last century the Society of Dilettanti, which had been founded in 1734, determined to send a mission to explore the ancient sites and remains of architecture and sculpture in Greece and Asia Minor. This mission, which consisted of Messrs. Chandler, Revett, and Pars, left England in 1764, and, after visiting Smyrna and other places on the west coast of Asia Minor, proceeded to Athens. The results of this first mission were recorded in *The Antiquities of Ionia*, Part I. published in 1769, and Part II. in 1797. In 1812 the Society sent a second Mission to Greece and Asia Minor under the direction of Sir William Gell, who was accompanied by the architects John Peter Gandy and Francis Bedford. The labours of this second Mission enabled the Society to publish, in 1817, a volume on *The Antiquities of Attica*, and in 1840 a third part of *The Antiquities of Ionia*. They also republished, in 1821, Part I. of the same work, with many additions and corrections. In 1851 the Society published Mr. Penrose's work on *The Principles of Athenian Architecture*, in which he has recorded his investigations as to the optical refinements which the Parthenon and certain other buildings at Athens possessed.

The discovery of the Smintheum in the Troad, which was made by Captain (now Admiral) Spratt in 1853, was one of the reasons which induced the Society to send a new expedition to the west coast of Asia. It was, moreover, felt that, having regard to the great advance in the knowledge of Ionic architecture which had been made since the first part of the *Ionian Antiquities* had been published, it would be desirable to explore more thoroughly the Temple of Athena Polias at Priene and that of Dionysos at Teos. Mr. R. P. Pullan, who had been associated with Mr. Newton, by the Foreign Office, in the Budrum expedition to assist him as an architect, was selected by the Society for this new mission, the results of which are given in the present volume. Mr. Pullan explored Teos in 1862, and in 1866 was again sent out to conduct excavations at Priene and the Smintheum. The Plates in the present volume are engraved either from Mr. Pullan's drawings or from photographs, with the exception of Plates III. and IV., the drawings for which have been kindly contributed to the volume by Mr. E. L. Falkener.

The whole of the Plates of this work have been engraved by M. J. Pouch, in Paris, under the superintendence of M. Chevignard, and have been executed with great care and artistic skill.

The text has been contributed by four members of the Society, and it will be understood that each of them is responsible only for that portion of it which bears his signature.

MEMBERS OF THE SOCIETY OF DILETTANTI, 1881.

TABLE OF CONTENTS.

LIST OF THE PLATES.

LIST OF THE WOODCUTS.

INTRODUCTION.

ON THE ORIGIN OF THE GRECIAN ORDERS OF ARCHITECTURE.

THERE are few events in literary history so remarkable as the manner in which in the middle of the fifteenth century the learned world suddenly awoke to the discovery of the long-neglected beauties of classical literature. It is true that it was not till after the fall of Constantinople, in 1453, that the scholars of Western Europe had many opportunities of mastering the language of the Greeks, so as to be able to appreciate the beauties of their literature as expressed in their own exquisitely harmonious tongue. But the works of the poets and orators of Rome they always had in their hands, and the language in which they were written was understood and indeed used by every educated person. Yet their excellences were neither seen nor valued, as we now know they ought to have been, till the sudden revival of classical learning which preceded, only by a short interval of time, the great outburst of the Reformation.

If, however, the scholars turned with delight to pore over these long-neglected treasures, the artists of that age rushed with even greater enthusiasm to the study of the remains of classical art. The architects of Europe threw aside, at once, the forms and traditions of their own beautiful and appropriate mediæval styles, and for more than three centuries devoted themselves exclusively to the study of the marvellous remains with which the Roman Emperors had adorned not only the capital, but almost every city of the Empire. During that long period all their energies were devoted, first to mastering the details of the Roman styles, and then, to a not very successful attempt to reproduce them, and in so doing to adapt them to the requirements of an age and a state of society different from that for which they were intended, and to which—except from their own inherent elegance—they can hardly be said to have been suited. In all these efforts, however, it was Roman taste and magnificence that was admired, and Roman forms and details that were copied. It was not till the publication of the first volumes of Stuart's Antiquities of Athens, in 1761 and 1787, that the learned practically became aware that Greece possessed a separate style of her own, more elegant and refined than anything that Rome had ever produced, and, though probably less flexible for modern purposes, far more worthy of study than the style that had so long exclusively occupied the attention of Europe.

Since the commencement of Stuart's publications the progress of the study of Greek architecture, though at first slow, has gone on steadily increasing, latterly in an almost geometric ratio, culminating in the German explorations at Olympia now in progress, one of the greatest undertakings of its class, attempted in the present age, and which promises to be among the most important in its results. During this long interval every known temple of the Doric order has been explored, and its plan and details measured and drawn with as much exactitude as the state of the ruins admitted of being done, and, what is almost equally important, these have all been published, with an amount of care and elegance of engraving which has not yet been devoted to any other group of architectural objects in any part of the world. So nearly complete indeed are all the preliminary steps of the investigation that the time has probably arrived when it may be possible to attempt a monograph of the Doric order, and if this were done and illustrated in a manner worthy of the subject it would form one of the most valuable contributions that could be offered to the history of architecture, for it can hardly be doubted that with its sculptured and painted accompaniments it was the most artistic form of expression of the most intellectual people known to have existed, either in ancient or modern times.

The Ionic order has not been so fortunate in its history or its historians. This arises partly from the comparative paucity of the examples—they are not by one half so numerous as those of the Doric order, and partly from the more complete state of ruin in which they now exist. More, however, is due to their geographical distribution. All the examples of the Doric order, with the one exception of the temple at Assos, are found in the comparatively settled countries of Europe, either in Greece itself, in Sicily, or in Magna Græcia, whilst nineteths of the Ionic Temples are found in the native country of the order, which is less easily accessible, and where from various causes its state has been such as to render leisurely investigation of the remains always difficult, and sometimes impossible. Still much has been accomplished, and more is being done, so that these Asiatic temples may eventually take rank with those of the Doric order, so far at least as relates to their historical value, as illustrations of architectural art. It may be true that the Ionic order does not possess the same exquisite purity, and cannot pretend to that sublimity of effect which the Doric seems capable of attaining; but the greater Asiatic Ionic temples exceed in dimension the European examples of the Doric order—with two exceptions,[1] which are not of a high class as works of art—and, when complete, probably surpassed them in elegance and richness of architectural detail, though they may have been inferior in their sculptured and painted subjects. It would consequently be most interesting if we were in a better position to institute a satisfactory comparison between them.

The Ionic temples of Europe, unfortunately, afford but little aid in the investigation. In it there are some three or four little temples of this order, exquisite in detail, like everything the Greeks ever did, but so small as only to be considered as cells, hardly deserving the name of temples. The one temple[2] of any considerable dimensions of this order is that of Minerva Polias, in the Acropolis at Athens, but even that is small, though of surpassing interest. In beauty of detail and the propriety with which its design is adapted to its intended purposes, there is, probably, no more beautiful building to be found anywhere. But it is so exceptional in plan and design, that it is only the details of its architecture that are of any assistance in an investigation of the history of the orders.

THE ORIGIN OF THE DORIC ORDER.

There are few points connected with the archæology of Greece that have, in recent times, been more fully, and, it may be added, more warmly, discussed than those involved in the questions as to the origin of this

---

[1] The two temples alluded to are the Temple of Jupiter, at Agrigentum, which is not a peristyle temple at all, and of singularly clumsy design; the other is that of Jupiter at Selinus, which is so ruined that its original plan can with difficulty be ascertained. If it were as restored by M. Hittorff, *L'Architecture Antique de la Sicile*, pls. 65 to 74, it was one of the least satisfactory designs ever perpetrated by a Greek architect.

[2] A seeming exception to this assertion will occur to every one at all familiar with the history of Grecian architecture, in the Temple of Minerva Alea at Tegea. This temple has hitherto been known only from Pausanias' description of it (book viii. chap. 45), and all the world have agreed that he describes it as externally adorned by a peristyle of Ionic pillars and internally with Corinthian pillars standing on others of the Doric order. This was so monstrous an arrangement, and so unlike anything else in Grecian architecture, that no one could accept it without trying to find some means of escape. None however at all plausible seems to have suggested itself, except by assuming that when Pausanias said ἐντός, he means ἐκτός, or that some ignorant copyist had substituted the one word for the other; this however, as involving an alteration of the text, was quite indefensible.

So the matter rested till Herr Bötticher was deputed by the German Government to examine the site. This he was able only partially to accomplish, as a village occupied the whole area of the temple, which he had not the means to purchase and remove. He ascertained however that its dimensions were 70 feet by 155, and among the ruins he found a fragment of a Doric column, whose profile exactly suited the peristyle of a ostyle temple of these dimensions. Having satisfied himself on this point, Bötticher then makes the suggestion (*Mittheilungen des Archäologischen Institut zu Athen*, 1st half, 1860, pp. 32 et seqq.) that probably the Ionic order was employed only in the pronaos and posticum, and the Corinthian in the interior, thus reducing the whole to order and beauty, and, what is most strange, in strict accordance with every word of Pausanias' description:—

ὁ μὲν δὴ πρῶτος ἐστιν αὐτῷ κόσμος τῶν κιόνων Δωρίου, ὁ δὲ μετ' τοῦτον Κορίνθιος· ἐνετσαν δὲ καὶ ἐκτὸς τοῦ ναοῦ κίονος ἐργασίας τῆς Ἰώνων.

Now that this solution is suggested, it seems passing strange that it never occurred to any of the commentators of Pausanias that in his description of the temple he used the word ναός in its re-stricted but perfectly legitimate sense as applicable to the cella or abytus of the temple only. But any one does this term never would have been a doubt about the arrangements of this temple. The position too of the Doric as the first and principal order ought to have made commentators pause before interpreting a temple which now turns out to have been architecturally more beautiful than any other we are acquainted with. As the case at present stands we now know that it was externally a Doric hexastyle temple with two or six Ionic columns in the pronaos and posticum, and with probably ten or eleven columns of the Corinthian order in the interior of the cella. The Ionic order consequently stands here in exactly the same relation to the Doric as it did in the Propylæa at Athens and elsewhere. For the whole of the interior columns to be in the Corinthian style was certainly preferable to the introduction of a single specimen of that order, at this or, in fact, the three orders do not seem to have been combined anywhere so happily as in this hitherto anomalous temple.

However right Pausanias may have been in his description of the temple, he certainly was wrong when he said it was the largest of Peloponnesian temples; he forgot the Temple of Jupiter at Olympia, which was nearly twice its dimensions. That temple covered—as nearly as can be ascertained from the plans—19,840 square feet, while this one at Tegea covers only 14,450. Even the Heraion of Elis covers 19,230, and certainly surpassed it in the number of its pillars and consequent apparent size.

order. Since the publication of the late Sir Charles Barry's drawings of the tombs at Beni Hassan, in 1825,[1] English architects have generally been inclined to admit that the Greeks derived the order from the so-called proto-Doric style of the Egyptians. On the Continent, on the other hand, writers seem inclined to resent this as a slur on the originality of the Greeks, and to insist that they invented every part of it; and that the whole was evolved from the primitive wooden architecture of their early ancestors. As generally happens in such cases, it is more a dispute about terms than about facts. The latter are now perfectly well known, and the inferences from them seem inevitable, though it is only now, it must be confessed, that we can write regarding them with the precision which is desirable in such cases.

Fortunately the steps by which the Egyptian order was evolved are clear, and can all be easily traced. There is, close alongside of the Sphinx, a temple, called that of Armachis, which is one of the very oldest buildings now known to exist in Egypt, anterior in all probability to the great Pyramids themselves, certainly more than 3000 years before Christ. The principal apartment in the temple or tomb is 33 feet in width, and consequently too wide to be roofed by single slabs. To remedy this it was necessary to divide it into three aisles.[2] This was effected by walls, not continuous, however, but interrupted by voids, alternating with piers which, in this instance, were somewhat longer in one direction than their breadth. On these were laid longitudinal beams of the same section as the piers, and on these again rested the transverse roofing slabs. The next step in the process was to make these piers an exact square in section, and in this form they are found in several tombs of the same age as the Pyramids.[3] The third was to chamfer off the angles so as to reduce the shaft to an octagon, only retaining a square block at the top as an abacus, a form which is first found at Beni Hassan[4] under the twelfth dynasty. Following up the same course, the Egyptians again cut off the angles so as to turn the octagon into a prism of sixteen, then of twenty-four, and lastly of thirty-two sides.[5] When, however, they had reached these two last high numbers, it became evident that the angle between the sides was so obtuse as to be almost undistinguishable, with flat surfaces, and to remedy this defect they counter-sank the faces with curvilinear grooves, in other words, fluted the columns. They thus arrived, as early certainly as the twelfth dynasty (2340 B.C.), at a circular, fluted column, crowned by a square abacus and supporting a square beam of a section about equal to its original modulus. These columns were also made tapering, but whether from a sense of beauty or because all Egyptian walls slope inwards is not quite clear.

We have thus all the principal elements of a Doric order introduced in Egypt certainly 1000 years before the earliest example of it found in Greece. The one point where the comparison rather halts is in the projection of the abacus beyond the top of the shaft on which it is placed, and the consequent necessity of introducing an echinus or some corresponding invention to support it, and to break the abruptness of the transition. That this was also effected in Egypt seems certain from the fragments of three capitals which Ed. Falkener found in the southern temple at Karnak.[6] (Woodcut No. 2.) Unfortunately none of them were found in situ, and it has been hinted that it may have been a base, which from its form it may safely be said is most improbable, though it is hardly worth while arguing the point. If the Greeks really adopted the suggestion of this order from the Egyptians, it is very improbable that it could be from examples so far south as Beni Hassan or in Nubia, where the proto-Doric form is now principally found; but from buildings at Naucratis, or places in the Delta, with which they were more familiar. In the alluvial plains of northern Egypt stone is rare, and the probability is that this unitangular pillar was most frequently erected with bricks or small stones, and in that case a heavy projecting abacus, with some sort of echinus moulding, becomes almost a necessity, either for construction or beauty. Be that as it may, all above the horizontal stone beam, representing the architrave in the Grecian order, is undoubtedly

[1] Gwilt's edition of Sir W. Chambers' Civil Architecture, vol. i. p. 58. London, John Weale, 1825.
[2] It is to be regretted that, although this building was discovered some twenty years ago, no plan or details of it have yet been published in such a form as to be available for scientific investigation. A tolerably correct plan of it, though on a very small scale, will be found in Burckhardt's Handbook of Lower Egypt.
[3] Lepsius, Denkmäler, vol. i. pls. xxi. xxiii. xxvi. and xxvii.
[4] Sir Gardner Wilkinson, Arch. of Ancient Egypt, pls. ii. and iii.
[5] The Indian architects followed the same process in the design of their pillars, but they repeated all these forms in the same pillar, leaving the base and above square, and between the two introducing octagonal forms, and then those of sixteen and thirty-two sides, and always reserving the whole with a bracket capital to support the architrave, forms which neither the Egyptians nor Greeks ever adopted.
[6] Museum of Classical Antiquities, vol. i. p. 72.

of Grecian invention. In the rainless climate of Egypt the roofs were always flat, formed either with massive slabs, as those of nine-tenths of the temples appear to have been, or with small round beams of timber laid side by side and crossing one another so closely as to be able to support a mud roof, as seems to be simulated in the tombs at Beni Hassan. In Greece the roof always required a slope to throw off the rain, and for this purpose it was necessary to introduce a triangular truss of firmly-framed carpentry, to support the heavy tiles or slabs of stone with which the roof was covered. It seems hardly to admit of doubt, that the triglyphs of the Doric order are neither more nor less than copies in stone of the ends of these wooden beams, that the metopes represent the spaces between them, sometimes, but not always filled in, in early times, and that the cornice is only the last slab or tile of the roof projecting one-third or one-fourth beyond the purlin that supported it. The pediments at either end are, of course, only sections of this purely Grecian form of roof, which, besides its greater beauty externally, was eminently suited to a country where large beams of timber were everywhere available, but could hardly have been introduced in Egypt where timber of a suitable class must always have been a rarity.

If the facts of the case are as just stated, it seems as unreasonable to assert that the Greeks copied the Doric order from the Egyptians, as to deny that they borrowed some of the more important elements of their order from the banks of the Nile. Had the so-called proto-Doric ever been used as a sacred or templar order, with the Egyptians, or had they consequently ever carried it to its legitimate completion, it is probable the Greeks never would have adopted it. As it was, it was an invention of the old dynasties before the eighteenth, and used by them in tombs and similar buildings only, and thrown aside by the eighteenth dynasty as unsuited for their purposes. What the Egyptian builders wanted for their great temples were plain surfaces on which they could display the wealth of colour in which they luxuriated. The multangular surfaces of the proto-Doric were singularly ill-suited for this, and all their pillars in their great temples are, with scarcely an exception, of a plain circular section. The truth of the matter was that in those early days, both in Egypt as in Greece, colour seems to have been considered as essential as form, at least in architectural decorations, and whatever was incapable of being so adorned was rejected. The Romans were, in fact, the inventors of monochromatic architecture. Neither Greece or Egypt knew anything of it, or ever recognised a building as complete till the effect of every essential part of it had been heightened by the application of colour. It was, most probably, in consequence of this defect that the proto-Doric column was rejected by the Egyptians in the great age, and because one of those waifs and strays of inchoate architectural design, which, just because they are but inchoate, any one is justified in appropriating and trying to carry to the degree of perfection of which they are legitimately capable. In this instance the original inventors seem to have neglected to bestow the requisite elaboration upon this order, because they had, in the meanwhile, invented other forms more suited for their purposes.

Whether this is or is not a complete explanation of the observed phenomena, it seems quite certain, at all events, that the Grecian Doric column, with its abacus and architrave, were not derived from any wooden original. We now know perfectly well, from our experience of Lycian tombs[2] and Indian cave temples,[3] what the process was by which a wooden style became converted into lithic architecture. At first, it is by copying literally every detail of the carpentry—the tenons, the mortices, even the pins and fastenings are all reproduced in stone, without any difference except in material. By slow degrees, sometimes after centuries, these wooden forms are gradually abandoned and replaced by others more suitable to the new material, but seldom, if ever, without leaving such reminiscences of their origin as to enable any one, accustomed to such inquiries, to detect at a glance their original parentage. Nothing of this sort can be detected in the Doric pillar or its architrave, and its existence would hardly have been suggested by any one who bears in mind that carpentry forms depend for their stability almost wholly on the constructive skill with which their various parts are combined and fastened together. Lithic forms, on the contrary, depend as exclusively on their mass and the consequent aid they obtain from the action of terrestrial gravity, and are generally—or ought to be—as in the Doric order, wholly independent of any constructive expedients to ensure their stability.

Notwithstanding all this, it is more than probable that the Greeks used wood in the construction of the earlier temples before they had either wealth or skill sufficient to employ stone for that purpose; and history lends some slight support to this view. Pausanias, for instance, describes the first temple at Delphi as a hut formed with branches of the laurel tree,[4] and describes another near Mantinea as formed of oak beams,[5] but if

[1] If we may trust Pausanias, book v. c. 10, it was Byzes of Naxos, who lived in the time of Alyattes (sic. 617-611), who first introduced the use of marble instead of tiles on the roofs of temples. Like most of the remote tradition however mentioned by that author, too much reliance not be placed on it. It is probable he may have introduced some improvements in the roofing arrangements, but the whole spirit of the tale supports a heavy roof of stone from its first invention.

[2] Sir Charles Fellows, Travels in Lycia, and Xanthus, Lycia Minora, plates passim, and examples in British Museum.

[3] Fergusson's History of Indian Architecture, pp. 41, 116; and Cave Temples of India, J. F. and James Burgess, London, 1880, pp. 20 et seq.

[4] Pausanias, lib. x. ch. 5, p. 810.

[5] Ῥοϊὸν δἐκα ἐρμηνεύειν καὶ ἀρχαιότατος τοὺς ἔλάχθηρα. Pausanias, lib. viii. ch. 10, p. 618.

his description is at all to be depended upon, more like the log hut of an American or Russian peasant than anything of the Doric order.[1] Nor is there anything, so far as is known, that would lead us to suppose that anything like a peristyle temple, or anything resembling the orders as we now know them, were at any time attempted in wood.[1]

Besides these wooden temples, however, the Greeks had, if one may trust Pausanias, others erected in bronze. The second temple at Delphi was, according to him, of that material,[2] and there are other indications of that metal being used for decorative purposes elsewhere. Fortunately we have one very ancient order in Greece that looks very much as if it were derived from a metal original, though of course it would now be in vain to look for any specimens of pillars in so valuable a material. Still the two pillars that adorned the entrance of the so-called Treasury of Atreus at Mycenæ[3] could only be derived from some such original. There is nothing lithic about them, nor anything that would suggest a wooden derivation, while the extent to which we know that bronze was employed in the interior of that treasury or tomb would strongly favour the idea that either metal or metallic forms might be employed to adorn the exterior. Their presence there, however, goes to prove, so far as a single instance can, that no Doric forms existed in Greece at the time these pillars were erected, nor anything at all approaching them either in form or in design.

The most convincing proof, however, that we have that the Doric pillars never could have been derived from a wooden original is from the fact that the oldest are the most solid and the most unlike wooden forms.

There is a group of temples, consisting of one at Corinth, the Temple of Neptune at Pæstum, and two at Syracuse, which are generally admitted to be the oldest examples of the order existing. Their date may extend to within the limits of the seventh century B.C. Their height is very little in excess of four diameters. From that date for a century and a half, the Greeks in their own country, gradually but steadily, went on increasing their relative height till the proportion culminated, in the Parthenon and other buildings of the great age, at five and a half diameters. It went on still increasing, but more slowly, for another century and a half, till it reached six diameters, and perished then under the enervating influence of the Macedonian dynasty. So true is this that on the continent of Europe, in Greece proper, the proportion between the diameter and height of any Doric column forms the best chronometric scale by which the relative age of any two temples can be ascertained. This rule, however, does not hold good for the island of Sicily, where, from the variety of materials employed, and local peculiarities, the forms of the column are as various as the plans of the temples, and seem to defy all attempts at classification. Their range, however, is not great; the stoutest being four and a half diameters in height, the most slender reaching only to five,[4] which is still below the

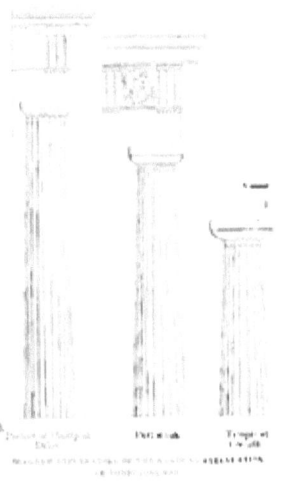

average of the best continental examples, and very far removed from anything that would suggest an origin derived from any possible construction in wood.

This being so, it seems almost impossible to conceive that any pillar derived from a wooden original, and consequently thin and attenuated, could have gone on increasing in massiveness during three centuries, till it attained proportions of more than lithic solidity; and that then, for three centuries more, the artistic energies of the Greeks were devoted to getting rid of the clumsy proportions it had attained, and that, after passing through perfection, the Greeks were at length forced to abandon it, because it had become so like a wooden post that the exquisite taste of the nation could no longer endure its attenuated proportions. There is not, so far as is known, any parallel for such up-and-down progress of any important member, in the architectural history of the world, and it seems impossible to conceive that it ever took place in Greece.

[1] The one thing in Pausanias that would recommend the idea of a wooden Doric order, is that in describing the Temple of Juno at Elis he mentions the existence of a wooden pillar in the posticum (lib. v. 16). As all the other pillars of the temple were of the Doric order, this one may have been so also in imitation of them, but there is nothing to show that this was so; and if it were, it would prove nothing, except that it was a cycle, or an imitative shaft which modems would very likely adopt, but would be most improbable in Greece.

[1] It was quite excusable in an amateur like Sir Clerke's Fellows to suggest that the peristyle temples of the Greeks were copied from the beautiful huts of the Lycian peasantry of the present day, but it does seem strange that an accomplished personal architect like M. Hittorff should devote all his ingenuity to elaborate such a theory (Architecture Antique de la Sicile, pp. 243, 246, pl. lxxx. to lxxxv.). It might be expected that at the present day such speculations would be relegated to the company at Mr. James Hall's attempt (Murray, 1813, octavo, 60 plates) to prove that all the decorative and constructive forms of Gothic architecture were derived from the interlacing of the branches of a grove of trees.

[2] Pausanias, lib. x. 5.

[3] Antiquities of Athens, supp. vol. i. ; Donaldson, Essays ; see also Gell's History of Greece, pls. lv. v. and vi. pp. 144 to 149.

[4] Hittorff, Architecture Antique de la Sicile, pl. 94.

c

It is now generally considered as an established fact among archæologists that the date of the earliest group of Greek Doric temples may be carried back to within the limits of the seventh century B.C., but no one has ventured to propose that even the archaic remains at Corinth can be dated earlier than the time of Cypselus, say 670 B.C. Notwithstanding this, it is impossible to suppose that such a temple, for instance, as that of Neptune at Pæstum, which if not quite is probably nearly as old, was the first attempt to carry out such a design. Its external order is so complete that, except in greater refinement, no essential alteration was made even in that of the Parthenon, and its internal arrangements are as natural as in any other temple we know of. There is nothing tentative about it. The same ordinance is found in the Temple of Jupiter at Ægina,[1] at least a century afterwards, and there is every reason to suppose it was repeated even in the Parthenon. Yet we ask in vain where are the earlier examples? Probably more than three or four centuries elapsed between the building of the Treasury of Atreus at Mycenæ and the erection of the monolithic columns at Corinth ; and during the greater part at least of that long period the Greeks were very nearly what they afterwards showed themselves to have been, and must have had temples of considerable magnificence—the order at Corinth is far too complete to be a first attempt— but of those no remains have been found from which the progress of the invention can be traced.

It may have been, as hinted above, that the proto-Doric of the Egyptians was carried forward to a much greater similarity with the Grecian order, in the Delta, to the north of Memphis, and to a greater degree of perfection than is displayed in the examples at Beni Hassan and in Nubia. It may consequently be, that when the Greeks first adopted it they may have used brick, or rubble-stone work, for the core of their pillars, as these northern Egyptians most probably did, and the earlier examples may consequently have perished by a natural process of decay. But from whatever cause it may have arisen, the loss is certain, and it appears is now irremediable, and if this is so, it is as much to be regretted as any other hiatus in the whole history of architectural art.

The application of the Doric order to the templar exigencies of the Greeks is a much simpler problem than the invention of the order itself, and hardly requires the mechanical evidence of examples to render its progress clear. Although there may have been, in some well-wooded parts of the country, wooden cells, in which the images of the gods were enshrined, as there were wooden parish churches in this country, they most have been rare. The country abounded in stone suitable for building purposes, and, from the time of the building of the Treasury at Mycenæ, long before any Image-temples existed, the Greeks had shown themselves perfectly capable of cutting stone with precision, and using it scientifically for architectural purposes.

The first form the earliest Image-temples took, was naturally and appropriately, a cell, square in plan, and probably a cube in dimensions internally. In these the light was admitted by the door and through that only. The first improvement in this simple cell was to protect this essential opening from the weather. This was

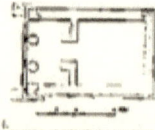

effected by producing the side-walls, and terminating them in antæ or square piers, and placing between them two round pillars of the Doric order, thus producing a crypto-porticus of great beauty and appropriateness. The next step appears to have been to free the antæ and to convert them into pillars, as was done in the temple of Empedocles, at Agrigentum,[2] making it tetrastyle ; and another was to repeat these four free standing columns behind the cell, as was done in the temple of Nike Apteros at Athens,[?] making it amphiprostyle. These two last-named temples are in the Ionic style, and it is doubtful whether, in very early times, these porticoes were introduced

into any temples of the Doric order ; what was adopted in that style was to repeat the crypto-porticus in the rear, so as to form an opisthodomos, as is found in the small temple at Eleusis. The free standing pillars in these small Doric temples were evidently introduced principally for ornament sake. They were not required so much by the constructive necessities of their position, as that they were indispensable for architectural effect. Without them the façades would have looked weak and poor to an inconceivable extent, while they hardly impeded the admission of light to the cella through the doorway, which it was their primary object to protect. It was probably, to ensure this that these simple temples always remained so small : that at Rhamnus was only twenty feet by thirty-two, and that at Eleusis twenty feet by forty over all.[?]

With these simple elements the Greeks produced one of the most perfect temple forms that had ever been invented. Its principal defects were, that from the paucity of the elements of which it was composed it hardly

---

[1] Cockerell's Ægina and Bassæ, pls. iii. to vi.   [?] Hittorff, Architecture Antique de la Sicile, pls. xvii. and xix.

[?] Principles of Athenian Architecture, Penrose, pl. xxvii.   [?] Antiquities of Attica, chapter vii. pl. i. ; and chap. v. pl. 3.

[?] Some fifty years ago a little Grecian Doric cell chapel in satin was erected at Calcutta, to contain a marble statue of Warren Hastings, and nothing more beautiful of its class is in its modern times been erected, or anything more appropriate to its purpose ; but even in that climate it was found expedient to omit the screen wall with its doorway, so that sufficient light should reach the statue, in order that it might be perfectly seen.

admitted of any progressive development, or of any additional magnificence, except by its increase in size, and that the Greeks seem always to have shrunk from, and artistically they were no doubt right. A magnified temple of Themis at Rhamnus would not have been more beautiful, and could hardly have escaped being vulgar.

The next step in the invention was a giant's stride; it consisted in placing six free-standing pillars in front of the crypto-porticos of the old form, and as many behind, and joining these two by a screen of pillars, twelve or thirteen, extending along the flanks, and so enclosing the whole of the old temple with its pronaos and posticum in a screen of columns, which thus became practically, in an architectural sense, the temple itself, as is shown in the annexed plan of the temple of Nemesis at Rhamnus. This, though neither one of the oldest or finest, is one of the most complete, and contains all the elements of the hexastyle Doric temple, which remained stereotyped during the whole of the great age of Greek architecture.

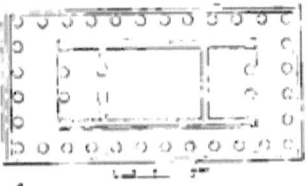

TEMPLE OF NEMESIS, RHAMNUS.

Strange though it may appear, it is nevertheless true, that we have no knowledge of the time when this capital improvement was introduced into the form of the Greek temples, nor any hint anywhere of even the traditional person to whom the invention was ascribed. Neither Pausanias nor Vitruvius nor Pliny refer to it as an invention at all; they seem to consider that Greek temples of certain dimensions were always peripteral, and, being unable to conceive any other state of things as ever existing, they did not care to inquire when the form was first introduced, but seemed to consider its origin as lost in the depth of primordial antiquity.

As the Greeks themselves have not cared to enlighten us on the subject, we naturally turn to Egypt to see whether the forms of any of the temples found there afford us any aid in our attempts to solve these problems. As it happens, we do there find a class of temples called Mammeisi, which have peristyles surrounding small cells, and in plan, at least, nearly identical with those afterwards erected in Greece. If Sir Gardner Wilkinson is to be depended upon, the use of these peripteral temples became rare after the middle of the eighteenth dynasty for reasons which he gives; but he sees no reason for doubting their existence from a very early age, down to about 1500 years B.C.[1] It is true they are now rare, but they were small and frail, and the materials of which they were composed singularly well suited, from their form, for appropriation to modern purposes. Sir Gardner quotes only three, but they may have been much more numerous, and the existence of only one, if its date were perfectly ascertained, would suffice for the argument.

If this were so, —though it must be admitted that the facts are hardly ascertained with sufficient precision to build much upon them,—the only logical inference would be that the Greeks saw this form in Egypt, and perceiving its adaptability for their own purposes borrowed it from that country, but applied it in their own, with a degree of originality and of appropriateness of detail which may well make us forget that it was not invented by the country where it grew to such an unrivalled degree of perfection.

There still remains one important question to which a satisfactory answer has yet to be suggested. Why did the Greeks adopt the peripteral arrangement? It was not wanted for any constructive purpose, nor even when perfected did it answer any mechanical conditions. It was not a verandah adapted to the protection of the servants of the temple, or loiterers from the weather. The space between the pillars and the wall was, in the best and earliest examples, too narrow to be suitable for processions, nor does it seem to have been arranged for that purpose. May it not have been that, struck with its beauty as employed in Egypt, the Greeks felt impelled to use it at home? Visitors to Egypt could hardly fail to be struck by the sublimity of the long colonnades, not only the hypostyle halls, but in the courts of the temples there, and may have sought to reproduce like effects in their own country.

Another suggestion that seems to meet the exigencies of the case is that the peristyle was adopted to protect the paintings on the external walls of the cella, and to heighten their effect by contrast with the plain whiteness of their own monochromatic fluted shafts. No one, probably, now doubts that the temples of the Greeks were richly coloured externally. The traces of it, that have been found in Sicily,[2] and even in the Parthenon itself[3] have quite set that question at rest. It is true the colour that has hitherto been found has only been on the architectural mouldings where they were protected from the weather, but it is impossible to conceive that the Greeks would have heightened one part of the temple so brilliantly and left other parts, where it was more required and more appropriate, as plain surfaces. In the whole temple there was no part so suited for a display of colour as the external walls of the cella. It was the only part, indeed, where anything like historical or figure painting could be introduced with effect, and it would be strange indeed if the Greeks did not avail themselves

[1] Sir G. Wilkinson, Arch. of Ancient Egypt, p. 72, pl. 1 fig. 29, 30, 31.

[2] Hittorff and Zanth, Architecture Antique de la Sicile, folio, Paris, 1870. Le Temple d'Empédocle à Sélinonte, 4to, 1851.

[3] Penrose, Principles of Athenian Architecture, pls. xxix. to xxxi.

of it for that purpose. As all these wall-paintings, if they existed, have perished from exposure to the weather during the last 2000 years, this cannot be proved directly, nor are we able, except by inference, to conjecture in what manner the subjects were treated. It almost certainly was not as one great composition treating of one connected subject, but must have been divided into numerous detached compositions, like those in the Lesché at Delphi[1] and elsewhere, each independent of the other, and whose effect would be rather heightened than destroyed by being separated from each other by the shafts of the columns of the peristyle. The manner in which the walls of apartments at Herculaneum and Pompeii are decorated, though belonging to a much more modern age, conveys to us now, perhaps, a better idea of the mode in which the walls of the cella of a Greek temple were decorated than any other known examples. It probably consisted, like them, of detached historical or sacred groups of more or less importance, interwoven with architectural decorations and relieved by the richly-coloured backgrounds of the panels in which they were placed.

There is one other argument which in itself seems almost conclusive on this point. If the Greeks did not want the external walls of their cellas as great surfaces for the display of paintings, they might easily have introduced a range of windows in their upper part so as to light the interior, as they did in the Erechtheum and the great Temple of Jupiter at Agrigentum. In the Parthenon, for instance, a range of openings immediately under the frieze, and extending nearly to the floor of the internal gallery,—if there was one,—would have admitted a sufficient amount of light, in a more artistic manner than has been done, in any modern building at all events. Externally such windows would have been perfectly protected by the peristyle from the weather, and internally nothing would have been so easy as to regulate the light by blinds or shutters from the gallery floor. Notwithstanding all this, we may say with certainty that neither in the Parthenon nor in any regular Doric temple elsewhere, was this obvious expedient for lighting the interior adopted; though we know from the neighbouring Erechtheum that the Athenians, at least, were not unfamiliar with the mode of lighting interiors by windows.

Instead of this, we may assume with very tolerable certainty that the Greeks, in all cases, admitted the light to the interior of their great temples through apertures in the roof. It has however been one of the most difficult problems connected with their architecture to ascertain how this was effected, but like many other mysteries it may by some be considered to have received at least a plausible solution from the German excavations at Olympia. According to an official report just published in Berlin,[2] it seems that the recent explorations in the great temple there have revealed the existence of, what the commissioners consider, to have been an inspluvium, constructed to receive the rain that fell through a hypæthron opening immediately over it. It is situated, as nearly as may be, in the middle of the cella, and is rather more than 20 feet square and 1 foot in depth, and is paved with black limestone surrounded by an edging of white marble. This however, and all that is said regarding it, corresponds exactly with the description found in Pausanias[3] of the tank situated immediately in front of the Chryselephantine statue, to contain the oil which it was thought necessary to place there for its protection, by counteracting the dampness of the locality in which the temple stood. So minute is this agreement that, until some further evidence is adduced, we may be allowed to hesitate before accepting the proposition that it served as an impluvium also. When however men so competent to form an opinion on such a subject, as the German commissioners undoubtedly are, confidently put forward such a theory, there seems no room, for the present at least, for disputing the conclusions they have arrived at. Assuming them, therefore, to be correct, an important gain from their explorations seems to be, that it may explain a passage in Vitruvius,[4] which has hitherto seemed hopelessly contradictory. It would make it appear that the two hypæthral temples he mentions —apparently the only two he was acquainted with—were the Parthenon at Athens and the Temple of Jupiter at Olympia. This, it is true, is a most unexpected conclusion to arrive at, for if there were any two temples in the whole of Greece which we would, "à priori," expect would be more carefully protected from the weather, than all others, it is the two which contained the marvellous Chrys-elephantine Colossi of Phidias.

It would by no means follow from this, that all Greek temples were lighted in this manner; on the contrary, from these being the only two quoted by Vitruvius, though in direct contradiction to his own definition, and

[1] Paintings in the Lesché at Delphi, by Polygnotus, illustrated by Riepenhausen. Memoirs of Classical Antiquities, vol. I, pls. I, and II.

[2] Herr Bœtticher Delphild, in the Berlin Anzeiger, 8 February, 1881. Notwithstanding the detailed form and confident tone of this report, it is understood that its conclusions are warmly contested at Berlin. To me it seems inconceivable that the Greeks should have adopted so barbarical a mode of introducing light to their temples, while others, mechanically so much more perfect, were available and known to them. It is fair, however, reasoning in the presence of ascertained facts, and if when all the particulars of the case are published in sufficient detail to enable others to judge of them it should turn out that Herr Bœtticher is justified in his conclusions, there is an end of the matter. In the meanwhile, however, we may perhaps be allowed to consider the case as "sub judice," though it is impossible to ignore statements so confidently put forward, to refuse to admit their cogency if their conclusions can be sustained.   • Pausanias, lib. v. ch. 11, p. 406.

[4] The difficulty with regard to the passage in Vitruvius (lib. iii. ch. 2) has arisen from his first describing correctly the example of Eupolis as octostyle and diptere, and then adding, "Hypæthros vero decastylos est in pronao et postico æthion vero eustylos." Of these he adds, "medium æmum sub divo est sine tecto." He concludes this paragraph by the contradictory statement, "Italia exemplar Romæ non est, sed Athenis octostylos, et in Templo Olympia," which, if it is new theory is correct, could only apply to the Parthenon and the temple at Elis, but one of these is hexastyle, the other octostyle, and neither are dipteral, nor have any affinity with temples of that class.

there being no others, except perhaps one at Epidaurus,[1] known to contain Chrys-elephantine statues, it may fairly be assumed that they were exceptional, while an examination of the peculiarities of those at Bassæ, Ægina, and Pæstum, would lead to the conclusion that a different mode of lighting was adopted in them. So far as can now be made out, it was by no opaion or clerestory above the upper range of columns.

There is still another peculiarity, which it is difficult to account for on any other hypothesis than the great value the Greeks set on these external wall paintings. Some of the later temples in Sicily are not only pseudo-dipteral, but the pteroma is widened at the expense of the cella ; their plan thus becomes abnormal,[2] and, judged from an architectural point of view only, it must be condemned as bad and unmeaning. But were it the fact, that at the time they were erected, the artists were ambitious of introducing larger and more continuous paintings on the walls, it became evidently of importance to provide the widest possible space from which they could be viewed, without any intervening pillars, and for this purpose their plans seem admirably adapted.

Whether these are or not the reasons that led to its invention, one thing, at least, is certain, that, once it was adopted, the Greeks never deviated from this hexastyle peripteral form. They varied the width and arrangements of the cella and of the pronaos and posticum, but, except in the Parthenon, and the great temple at Agrigentum,[3] they adhered to it with a tenacity that is remarkable in so imaginative a people. But they probably were right, and if we could see one of these temples with all its sculptures and paintings complete externally, and its cella furnished with all the requisite art, and lighted in the perfect manner we know they must have been, we too might be forced to confess that nothing so perfect of its class had been seen before or since ; and that the Greeks were right in adhering to forms so beautiful in themselves, and which had become sacred in their eyes from their being long devoted to the service of their gods.

THE ORIGIN OF THE IONIC ORDER.

There is probably no one who is at all familiar with ancient architecture of Central Asia, who will hesitate in admitting that the Ionic order was derived from the architecture of the Assyrian Empire, with even greater certainty than the Doric can be said to have owed its origin to works of the Ancient Egyptians. The reasoning, however, on which this conclusion is based, is of a totally different character from that which was advanced to show that the slater order was derived from the proto-Doric style still found on the banks of the Nile. In Egypt we can trace how the simplest possible forms of an architecture of stone piers and beams, almost wholly without ornament, were gradually, in the course of centuries, being moulded into one of multangular pillars and complicated epistylia, so similar to that afterwards found in Greece, that we can hardly refuse to admit the affiliation. In Assyria, on the contrary, we have absolutely no stone architecture, properly so called, before the time of the Achæmenidæ, probably nothing that can even be dated so far back as the reign of Cyrus, while there is every reason to believe that it was from their conquest of Egypt and of the Greek colonies of Ionia that the Persians first learnt to prefer stone to wood for their ornamental architectural forms.[4]

The knowledge we have acquired during the last forty years from the excavations of Layard and others enables us to assert, with very tolerable confidence, that the flat roofs of the Assyrian palaces were supported, like those of Solomon's buildings at Jerusalem, by pillars of cedar or some other wood, as suitable for the purpose ; most probably some species of pine, which we know from the sculptures abounded in the countries to which they had access. It certainly was some wood which would burn easily, as all the palaces seem to have been destroyed by fire, and was of so perishable a nature, when it escaped that danger it could not resist the decay of subsequent ages. Our only knowledge consequently of its forms is derived from the fact that when the Achæmenidæ undertook the building of their palaces at Persepolis and Susa, they copied literally in stone the forms that had been used in wood by their predecessors at Nineveh and Babylon.[5]

[1] Pausanias, lib. v. ch. 11, p. 402.　　　[2] Hittorff, Architecture Antique de la Sicile, pls. xxi. xxx. iii. and lxiii.

[3] The Temple of Ceres at Eleusis is not an Imageo-temple properly so called, but a Mystery Hall, and adapted specially for the celebration of the Eleusinian mysteries. It is, in fact, a literal translation into the forms of Grecian architecture of the great Hypostyle Hall of Karnac, and nearly as many by, or one-half its dimensions. The Temple is a square, measuring rather more than 166 feet (List of Antiq. ch b. pl. 3.) The Hall is a hollow square, measuring according to Leake 170 feet by 355 feet, a coincidence that could hardly be accidental under any circumstances. The arrangement too of the pillars and the mode of lighting the two halls is practically identical. The opinion of the Grecian, corresponding as exactly with the clerestory of the Egyptian example, as the difference of the two styles of architecture will admit of—a circumstance in itself almost sufficient to settle the question as to how light was admitted to meet at least of the Temple of the Greeks.—See True Principles of Beauty in Art, pp. 365 et seq. History of Architecture, woodcuts 22, 23, and 152, 153.

[4] Of course it is not to be supposed that the Assyrians did not use stone masonry for their city walls and gates, for terrace formations and foundations, for everything in short that can come under the head of Engineering as contra-distinguished from Architecture.

[5] The argument on which this assertion rests is too long to be attempted here, but is worked out in detail by me in The Palaces of Nineveh and Persepolis Restored, published by John Murray in 1851.

It is, consequently, from this comparatively modern, but fortunately little form, of Assyrian art, that we must work backwards; first, to ascertain what its earlier forms were, when the Ionians first came in contact with it, and to estimate the extent of the influence it may have exerted in the invention of the Ionic order. It is not, it must be confessed, either a satisfactory or a very logical mode of proceeding, nor one we probably would be obliged to have recourse to, but from the accident that all the Greek temples in Asia Minor were destroyed during the Persian wars under Darius and Xerxes. So complete, indeed, has the destruction been, that hardly a fragment of the order has been found in Asia Minor that can, with certainty, be dated as belonging to a period anterior to the Persian wars; yet it is certain that the Ionian Greeks had temples, and temples presumably built in stone, long before that period. It is probable, indeed, that some parts of the Temple of Juno at Samos may belong to the temple commenced by Rhœcus[1] about 600 years before Christ, and there is little doubt that if Sard's were properly explored numerous remains would be found of earlier temples, but till some well-authenticated fragments are brought to light, we must be content with speculations of a more or less satisfactory nature.

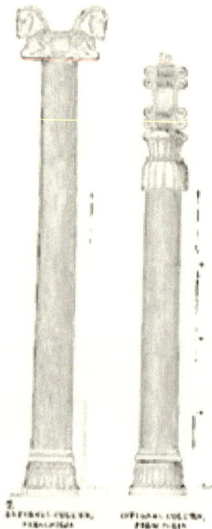

2. ASSYRIAN COLUMN, PERSEPOLIS.   OPTIMUS COLUMN, FROM PARIS.

Assuming therefore, for the nonce, that the Persepolitan order fairly represents the earlier forms of the architecture of Nineveh and of Central Asia, it is not difficult to trace the steps by which the Ionian Greeks sought to modify it into an order more suitable to their own principles of design, and more in harmony with their own beautiful Doric, which, whatever Vitruvius may say to the contrary,[2] was throughout, the true temple order of the Greeks. In the first place, they adopted the shaft almost literally. When used externally this was about ten and a half diameters in height without capital or base; as an internal column it was only about six and a half, but then it had an exaggerated capital and a tall base, so as to make the whole equal to the external order. Whichever form was employed, the shaft itself was adorned with forty or forty-eight flutes with fillets, and of a form very similar to those used in the perfected Ionic; and the diminution of the shaft was very nearly the same as that afterwards adopted. The Greeks never, unfortunately, adopted the Persepolitan bell-shaped base, which is one of the most pleasing features of the style. Perhaps they thought it too lofty, being about one diameter in height, and of course they never adopted the double-bull capitals of the external order. Its form was antagonistic to their principle of design, and in fact hardly excusable except in wood, or where it had a religious symbolism, which, in this instance, the Greeks did not share. In lieu of this they set themselves to modify and simplify the volutes of the internal capitals, so as to be able to use them externally and in harmony with the Doric principles of design; and they succeeded in accomplishing this with a degree of perfection, which all subsequent ages have acknowledged. What they invented was neither a notch capital, like that formed of double-bulls, which was not required in their mode of constructing roofs, nor a bracket capital, like that used by the Indians, which in Greek hands might have been an improvement; but it had this advantage over the Doric capital, that it had contrasted faces. In so monumental an order as the Doric, it is perhaps not a defect that all the four sides of the capital are the same, but in a more ornamental order it certainly is conducive to variety and elegance that the sides should be designed so as to be specially appropriate to their different positions. The flat faces of the volutes, extending either way beyond the shaft and merging with the architraves, suggest a bracket capital, without mechanically effecting it, and except at the angles, make a more perfect and complete design than can be produced by the simpler elements of the Doric.

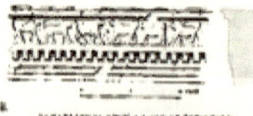

3. ENTABLATURE FROM A LION AT PERSEPOLIS.

The mode in which the inventors of the Ionic adopted the entablature of the Persepolitan order to their own uses was quite as ingenious. As will be seen from the annexed woodcut No. 8, it consisted of three parts. First an architrave resting on the great transverse beams which were laid at right angles in the hollow of the double-bull capital, which was rejected as having no analogue in Greek construction. This architrave consisted of apparently three thicknesses of timber, a number which was afterwards adopted by the Ionians. On this were laid the rafters

[1] Herodotus, iii. 60. The data on which its date is fixed are discussed and conclusions drawn with care in Smith's Dictionary of Greek and Roman Biography, in the articles on Rhœcus, Theodorus, and Telecles, they probably contain all that is known on the subject.

[2] Vitruvius, lib. iv. ch. Ph.; "Nonnulli antiqui Architecti negaverunt Dorico genere ædes sacras oportere fieri, ... itaque negauit Tuchesius, item Pytheus, non minus Hermogenes. Nam is cum parasset ingentem marmoris copiam in Dorica ædis perfectionum transtulit ex eadem copia et eam Ionicam Libero Patri fecit."—lib. iv. 3.

about their own width apart; these supported the planks on which were laid the mud or concrete that formed the flat roof, the edge of which was relieved by a procession of animals or urns. There was no cornice, of course, in this order, as it could not be constructed with the same material as the roof, and eaves were impossible with flat roofs. All that was wanted there was a device to collect the rain-water, and a cymatium forming a gutter with spouts to regulate its discharge. In utilizing the parts of this entablature, the Greeks left the architrave very much as they found it, and adopted the rafter ends as their modillion course, without essential alteration. But they took the liberty of transposing the zophorus from above the rafters, where it properly represented the edge of the roof, to a position above the architrave, where it ranged perfectly, it is true, with the metopal band of the Doric order, but had no constructive significance. Above the modillions they introduced a cornice of about the same projection as that used with the Doric order, and above that a cymatium, all which with a sloping, stone-roofed temple was not only appropriate but added immensely to the beauty of the whole design.

By all these changes the Asiatic Greeks may be said to have invented—they certainly perfected—an order which will hold its own with even that one invented by their European brethren. It may not be so pure, nor so monumental as the Doric, but in grace and elegance, both of proportion and detail, it would be difficult to surpass it by any architectural achievement in any other part of the world.

Unfortunately there do not appear to be any data available from which we can ascertain with anything like precision, at what time, the transformation of the Assyrian wooden style into the Ionic order of the Greeks took place. There is no passage in any work that has come down to us that even hints at such a thing, or connects any name with its invention. This, however, was hardly to be expected, as the change was probably so gradual that no one, at the time, noted, still less recorded it, for the benefit of future generations.[1]

The one passage that seems to bear, though somewhat indirectly, upon the subject, is the description in Pausanias of the Treasury which Myron, King of the Sicyonians, erected at Olympia, in the thirty-third olympiad (B.C. 648). This he describes as consisting of "two chambers constructed in bronze, one chamber being ornamented in the Doric the other in the Ionic style."[2] There is no description of their form, and no mention of pillars, or of any other architectural features; and we are consequently left very much to conjecture as to what their appearance was, and in what the distinction between the Doric and Ionic forms may have consisted. In the first place, it seems impossible that this brazen house was a square cell with a door probably covered by a portch, like the other treasuries uncovered by the Germans in their recent excavations at Olympia. The probability seems rather to be that it was a circular tholus with two corridors, like the so-called Treasury of Atreus at Mycenae.[3] That, as we know, was lined with plates of bronze internally, and the decoration of its exterior may fairly be considered of the Ionic order. The capitals of the pillars outside most probably had volutes, and the spiral decorations of the whole certainly were derived from an Asiatic source.[4] It is more difficult to determine how the Doric style was represented in Myron's Treasury. A pillar and epistylia of that order in bronze would be no anomaly that a Greek could hardly perpetrate, but a square fret and some conventional details from the order may have made the distinction evident to the practised eye of a Greek without the necessity of introducing pillars, which are the only means by which we now distinguish between them. It is

[1] In the third volume of Texier's Asie Mineure, and in Sir Charles Fellows' Excursion in Asia Minor and Travels in Lycia, there are between thirty and forty plates representing about one hundred rock-cut sepulchres both in Lycia and elsewhere in Asia Minor. Anyone who has access to these works or to the specimens in the British Museum can easily trace all the steps by which the carpentry forms of an architecture purely in wood were gradually elaborated into an Ionic order; rude, it must be confessed, but still as complete, in all essentials, as any examples of this order that were ever used by the Greeks even in the best age.

Precisely the same phenomena occurred in India at a slightly later epoch also. In probably was from their coming in contact with the Greeks established in the tritriorial that the Indians in the reign of the great Asoka (B.C. 250) first undertook to repeat the carpentry forms of their sacred buildings in the rock. This they did even more literally than the Lycians, as they continued to use wood in conjunction with stone for a considerable period. It probably was owing to their not being in immediate contact with any people using stone architecture that the process of conversion was so slow; but it can hardly be said to have been complete ten centuries after Asoka's times, when the Buddhist style disappeared with that religion from India in the seventh century of our era.

There is no evidence to show how long the process lasted in Lycia; it probably was much more rapid there, possibly not lasting more than a couple of centuries. Situated however as the Lycians were, they could not have been entirely ignorant of the use of stone for ornamental architectural purposes by the Egyptians, Greeks, and Persians, long before and during the time they were repeating their wooden forms in stone, and they could consequently hardly long resist the influence of their more advanced neighbours. Hist. of Arch. vol. ii. p. 47, et seq. Cave Temples of India, p. 29 et passim.

[2] Pausanias, lib. vi. ch. 19, p. 497.

[3] Gell's Journey to Greece, pls. iv. v. vi. and vii. Professor Donaldson in Antiquities of Athens, sup. vol. pls. iii. iv. and v. There, as in most instances, the capitals are represented as of a quasi-Corinthian order, but wholly without authority. All the evidence available seems to point to a primitive form of Ionic as more probable.

[4] If this conjecture is at all correct, it is probable that the origin of this treasury may still be found buried in the great mound that still exists to the northward of the Heraeum at the base of Mount Kronion. The Germans seem to have dug a slight trench into it (Ausgrabungen zu Olympia 1877-78, part iii. pl. xxx.) but to have abandoned it, having found nothing. I wish they had dug a little deeper.

hardly, however, worth while to speculate on these points in this place ; what we learn from the passage is, that in the middle of the seventh century B.C. the distinction between the Doric and Ionic orders was so perfectly well understood that no special definition was considered necessary to render the fact intelligible to others.

There is nothing, indeed, at all improbable that the distinction between the two orders was well known at least as early as this, inasmuch as we learn from Herodotus that the great Temple of Juno at Samos was erected by an architect named Rhœcus, whom we may assume to have lived about, but not earlier than 600 B.C. This temple Herodotus compares with the labyrinth of Egypt and the temple at Ephesus for extent and magnificence,[1] and states that it was the largest he had seen.[2] The remains now existing on the spot go far to confirm this last assertion, though they are so scattered that it is not now easy to ascertain what its dimensions actually were. The details given by Mr. Belford would apparently make it 167·6 feet wide by 362 feet in length.[3] But it was recently examined by Mr. Paul Girard,[4] who makes the front only about 165 feet and does not attempt to ascertain its other dimensions, but according to his figures they seem to have been something less than those just quoted. The truth, however, cannot be ascertained without excavation, but there seems no place where it would be more easy to undertake this, or where the results would be more interesting. It is more than probable that the pillar now standing, but without its capital, belongs to the temple Herodotus saw and described. In diameter it surpasses any pillar now found in Asia Minor, being 6 feet 5·4 inches, which would be quite suitable to a temple of the largest size, and the form of the bases throughout is singularly archaic, and by no means beautiful.[5] They consist of a circular drum with six or seven parallel horizontal flutings without any subordination among themselves. These are surmounted by a fluted torus moulding, which is almost certainly borrowed from Persia, as a similar one is found at Passargadæ attached to the tomb of Cyrus,[6] and probably, therefore, of the time of Cambyses, as no such base is found in Greece in that, or, indeed, in any early age. Be this as it may, the point that most interests us here is, that the Asiatic Greeks, probably as early as the year 600 B.C., were capable of undertaking the erection of a stone temple of the Ionic order, on a scale which they never surpassed, perhaps never equalled, in so far as its peristyle was concerned. If this were so, not only the order, but the whole templar ordinance must have been long familiar with them, and must have gradually grown to completion during several preceding centuries.

TEMPLE AT EPHESUS.

Although Herodotus is probably correct when he asserted that the temple at Samos was the largest Greek temple that he had seen,[1] it is not clear that he would not have modified this opinion had he lived after the time of Alexander and seen the last form which the temple at Ephesus took. The temple he saw there was that afterwards burnt by Herostratus on the night Alexander was born (356 B.C.), and it was probably unfinished at his time. It is true Mr. Wood's researches would lead us to suppose that the last three temples there, were on the same spot, and probably of the same dimensions, or nearly so, but it was not in its peristyle only that the great glory of the Ephesian temple resided, though it was only in that respect that it admitted of comparison with that at Samos.[2] If we know the exact dimensions of the Samian temple, which is doubtful, the latter was four feet wider (167 against 163), and about twenty feet longer (362 against 342); but that at Ephesus stood on a stylobate ten feet in height, and measuring, according to Pliny, 220 Greek feet by 425;[3] and it most probably was from the mode in which this podium, "universum templum," was ornamented with sculptured bassi rilievi, and adorned with statues either singly or in groups, that the temple owes its greatest fame, and from which it came to be considered one of the seven wonders of the world.

The one peculiarity that seems to distinguish this temple from all others we are acquainted with, is that thirty-six of its pillars were sculptured—one of these by Scopas.[4] What this meant was long a puzzle to

[1] Herodotus, iii. 60.   [2] Herodotus, ib. ii. 148.

[3] Antiquities of Ionia, vol. i. p. 61. They are there stated as 314 by 165 feet, but it seems to have omitted to take into account the dimensions of the angle columns.

[4] Bulletin de Correspondance Hellénique, pp. 384-91. Athens, June, 1880.

[5] Antiquities of Ionia, vol. i. ch. v. pl. ib. iv. and v.   [6] Flandin and Coste, vol. iv. pl. 197. Texier, vol. ii. pl. lxxxiii.
[7] Lib. ii. ch. 60.

[8] These particulars, and indeed all we really know about this long lost temple, are derived from the work, Discoveries at Ephesus, published by Longmans in 1877, in which Mr. Wood describes the researches he carried on during eleven long years with such indomitable perseverance on the site of this temple. It is very much to be regretted that he has not since found an opportunity of publishing the detailed plan which he possesses of his discoveries or a specification of where the various objects were found. The plan in his work above alluded to is on too small a scale and too indistinct is should to be of any use for reference purposes; and till a larger plan is published or a copy of it at least deposited in the British Museum many important facts connected with his researches must remain unknown to the public. By the aid of an incomplete copy of his plan, which he kindly lent me, I was enabled to work out several of the problems involved in his discoveries, but in a much less satisfactory manner than could have been done had all the necessary information been then available. Such results as I obtained were published in the Sessional Papers of the Institute of Brit. Arch. for 1877.

[9] Pliny, Hist. Nat. lib. xxxvi. 14.

archæologists, but is now made clear by Mr. Wood's explorations, and the fact that several drums so treated are now in the British Museum. The greater number were carved with one range of figures, nearly life size, like those in the Elgin room there, but several—probably eight—four in the pronaos, and four in the posticum, were raised on square pedestals, similarly sculptured, of which several examples have likewise been brought home.[1] These, however, though no doubt beautiful objects, would not, in themselves, be sufficient to render this temple a "wonder of the world"; nor would its hundred columns, which were, according to Pliny,[2] 60 Greek feet, or as nearly as may be ten diameters in height; nor, in fact, is there anything in the temple itself which would entitle it to that distinction. If, indeed, there was not something in its stylobate which rendered it quite different from ordinary Greek temples, the application of that name is as mysterious now as it was before the late discoveries. There can, however, be little doubt that the "universum templum" of Pliny was adorned in a manner which distinguished it from all other Greek temples, and rendered it worthy of the admiration it excited.

Although we know that the period of the greatest activity in building the last and greatest of the temples at Ephesus was probably, the time when Alexander visited the place (B.C. 334), and offered to pay the whole expense of the restoration if allowed to inscribe his name upon it, and when Scopas flourished, it is not so easy to ascertain when it was begun, and when finished. Pliny gives us two dates, which, at first sight, it is difficult to reconcile: the first is, that its erection occupied all Asia for 120 years;[3] the second is, that 400 years were spent in this undertaking, in like manner, by the whole of Asia.[4] The probability seems to be that the first statement refers to the last temple only, and dates from the time when the penultimate temple was burnt by Herostratus, in the year when Alexander was born (B.C. 356), as it can hardly be doubted that, immediately after that disaster, the Ephesians would set about restoring their damaged fane, whilst its complete rebuilding might very well have lasted till 236 B.C.

If we assume that the 400 years—evidently a round number—date backward from the year of its completion, they will carry us back to about 636 B.C., and would include the three last temples, which, from Mr. Wood's discoveries, we know were so like one another in every respect, that they may well have been considered as the same temple, which, though twice damaged by fire was restored in the same form on the same spot. This theory would accord perfectly with what we are told happened when Crœsus besieged the place (in 562 B.C.),[5] when the temple was certainly on this site, seven stadia from the city walls. It would also include the temple, so much admired by Servius Tullius (B.C. 557) that he determined to erect a copy of it at Rome.[6] It carries us back also to the age of Rhœcus and Theodorus, in whose time it seems certain the temple was erected on a new site, different from that of the older temples. If this had not been the case, we should not have had a description of the new foundations, laid on sheepskins and charcoal, but as the layer of charcoal was found in Mr. Wood's excavations it confirms the belief that about this time new foundations were put in on a new site.[7]

TEMPLE AT BRANCHIDÆ

In so far as its columnar arrangements were concerned the Temple of Apollo at Branchidæ, near Miletus, in many respects excelled its Ephesian rival. It had 120 pillars instead of 100, and they were as elegant in form and 3 feet taller. It is true this excess in number added very little to the external appearance of the temple, as it arose, first from the front being decastyle instead of octastyle, and consequently requiring four pillars between the antæ in the pronaos and posticum; to these must be added twelve internal pillars in the pronaos, which hardly added to the external effect. The two at each front and one additional pillar

[1] Mr. Wood assumes that these formed part of the frieze; they are however much too solid for that purpose, and besides they present five angles between sculptured faces, whereas there could only be four such, in the frieze of the temple, even supposing that by some strange accident the four angle stones alone had been found, and no other fragments of the frieze. Besides this, several show the marks of a circular drum on their upper surface which seem quite sufficient to settle the question. Mr. Wood's idea that three circular sculptured drums were placed in some instances one over the other seems untenable from any evidence obtained, besides being objectionable from an artistic point of view.

[2] Pliny, *Hist. Nat.* xxxvi. 14.   [3] Pliny, *Hist. Nat.* xxxvi. 14.

[4] Pliny, *Hist. Nat.* xvi. 40. In attempting to reconcile these two very discrepant numbers I have adopted the suggestion of Salmasius (*Pliu. Exercit.* § 577, who states that in several ancient manuscripts 120 is written for 220, which is found in the majority. I am perfectly aware of the danger of tampering with the text of a book, but if it ever was justifiable it is where an author adds two such different dates to a well-defined fact described almost in the same words (book xvi. "cum tota Asia extruxisse quadringentis annis peractum sit"); book xxxvi. "ducentis viginti annis factum a tota Asia"), and I am not aware that any one has suggested any plausible mode of reconciling them; till the Ichnom we are probably justified in adopting a hypothesis which agrees perfectly with the known facts of the case as ascertained from other sources, and has at least some written grounds for its support.

[5] Herodotus, i. 26.   [6] Livy, i. 45. *Auc. Vict. de Viris Illust.* vii. 9.

[7] *Ding. Laert.* ii. 8.

on each flank certainly were additions. Whether they balanced in effect the wide and graduated spacing of the Ephesian front is a question more difficult to determine. The spacing of all the pillars on the front and flanks of the Didymean temple was the same. At Ephesus the two central columns were 28 feet 8 inches apart from centre to centre, and bore, consequently, one of the largest architraves ever known to have been used. The next two were 23 feet 6 inches, the next 20 feet 4, and the outer 19 feet 4, while the spacing on the flanks was 17 feet 2, or a fraction less than that of the Didymean temple throughout.

One of the results of some excavations made at Branchidæ in 1873 by MM. Rayet and Thomas,[1] was the discovery that the bases of eight columns of the principal front were richly ornamented with sculptures of conventional designs, not of course to compare with that of the "columnæ cælatæ" of the Ephesian temple, nor even with the sculptured bases of Persepolis or Susa, but more as a reminiscence of these latter. In designing them the architect has sought to retain the general outline of the Grecian Ionic base, instead of boldly adopting the eastern form, which certainly, in this instance, would have been an improvement.

It is still a matter of uncertainty what the form of the entablature of the order of this temple may have been. There are still two columns standing, and they bear between them a fragment which has generally been assumed to represent the architrave, but it is so narrow that, if the other parts were in proportion, the entablature would only have been a little more than 10 feet in height, and consequently only one-sixth of that of the pillars, according to the plates published in the first volume of the Ionian antiquities,[2] and Texier arrives at the same conclusion.[3] The fact, however, is that restorers have hitherto failed to observe that this so-called architrave is a part of the internal, not of the external, order of the temple, and its height depends on the arrangement of the lacunaria of the internal roof, and has no reference to the external form of the building. If MM. Rayet and Thomas found anything bearing on this point they have not yet communicated it to the public.[4] In the meanwhile, however, so far as any evidence yet published is concerned, it may safely be assumed that the entablature of this temple was not less in proportion to the order than elsewhere, or about one-fourth that of the pillars, or from 15 to 16 feet without any cymatium. The pillars themselves are nine and three-quarter diameters in height.

Practically the width of the Didymean temple is identical with that of the temple at Ephesus, though the former is somewhat longer, from the introduction of an extra pillar in the flanks, probably to accommodate some internal arrangement, the significance of which, from its ruined state, we cannot at present perceive.[5]

[1] Gazette des Beaux Arts, Avril, Juillet, et Septembre, 1876.
[2] Ant. of Ionia, vol. i. ch. iii. pls. iv. and vi.
[3] Texier, L'Asie Mineure, vol. ii. pl. 137, &c. Pullan, Principal Ruins of Asia Minor, pl. iv.
[4] If MM. Rayet and Thomas had not shown such haste to anticipate the publication by the Dilettanti Society of the results of the excavations made at their expense at Priene, they might long ago have given to the world the results of their own interesting explorations of this temple. As it is, the papers published by them in the Gazette des Beaux Arts are only sufficient to whet the appetite, but are too jejune sufficient to satisfy the craving for information on this most interesting subject.
[5] One of the most striking peculiarities of these Ionian temples was the frequency of their being destroyed by fire. Of course it is not to be wondered at that a temple such as that at Branchidæ should have been so destroyed by the Persians. When a hostile army invades a country, burning the people and despoiling their gods, the destruction of their temples follows as a matter of course; the sleepless mode of effecting this is, obviously, to accumulate faggots and other combustible materials in their interior and to set fire to them. By this means not only is the woodwork of the roof consumed, but the walls, if of marble, so calcined as to render their restoration almost impossible otherwise than by complete rebuilding. The case however was different with the Ephesian temple. The destruction of the penultimate temple there was the act of an unskilled incendiary in 356, and we have nothing but a somewhat apocryphal story in Eusebius, who tells us that the previous temple was accidentally burnt in 399 B.C.; it, as stated above, was probably erected about the year 600 B.C.; but before that date, if we may trust the expression of Pliny, "septies restituta templo,[?]" there were four earlier temples to Diana at Ephesus, all of which apparently shared the same fate. The first, about the year 1300 B.C., was burnt by the Amazons, according to Callimachus, about 1350[?]. The burning of the second temple is mentioned incidentally by Clemens Alexandrinus with that of the third. The fire that burnt the temple at Argos with Chryses the priest, also burnt the Temple of Diana, which is in Ephesus the second time after that of the Amazons.[?] The fourth temple was burnt by Lygdamis in the reign of Ardys II. King of Lydia (680-631 B.C.) The fifth and sixth, as mentioned above, shared the same fate. The seventh, following the words of Pliny, was "restituta," but, fortunately for us, never suffered from fire.

Notwithstanding the frequency of these burnings, we should hardly be justified in assuming that even the earliest of these temples were erected wholly of wood; but, coupled with the total disappearance of all the earlier temple in Asia Minor, it does seem probable that wood was employed to a greater extent, especially in the interiors, than was the case in Doric buildings. We hardly need anywhere of Doric temples accidentally destroyed by fire; indeed it is not very easy to see how either an incendiary or an accident could set fire to such a temple as the Parthenon, or to any of the great Sicilian temples; though a barbarian army could, of course, effect their destruction by that means without difficulty.

It is probable that in the first Ephesian temple, the architect, warned by experience, reproduced in incombustible materials the form which in earlier examples may have been in wood; but from the present state of our knowledge it seems fair to assume that the Ionic order was not only copied from a wooden original, but was used with wooden adjuncts to a greater extent than was the case with the Doric or any other style of Grecian architecture.

[*] Eusebius Pamph. Chronicon, Pseudo-, i. 134.   [†] Hist. Nat. xvi. 40.
[‡] Euseb., loc. cit. ii. p. 85. I am indebted to Falkener's Temple of Rome, p. 221 et seq. for these references. He seems thoroughly to have exhausted the subject.
[§] Works, Oxford edition of 1755, vol. i. p. 47.

Indeed, there are few things regarding these greater temples of the Greeks more remarkable than the close approach to identity of their dimensions, though differing so remarkably both in age and design, as well as in the locality where they are found. Practically they are double squares in plan, with one side measuring 165 to 170 Greek feet or thereabouts, though what there should be in these numbers to govern their design it is difficult to divine.[1]

TEMPLES AT SARDIS AND MAGNESIA.

The Temple of Cybele at Sardis, ranks next in importance among Ionic temples after the three just mentioned as existing at Samos, Ephesus, and Didyme. It has unfortunately not been explored to any extent. Three of its columns are still standing, and two of them have an architrave, while the frusta of several others protrude through the soil which covers the floor of the temple to a depth of about twenty feet. From these, Professor Cockerell, in 1819, ascertained the extent of the front to be 143 feet 4 inches, and found it to possess the same wide intercolumniation in the centre, and the same graduated distances towards the flanks that characterised the temple at Ephesus. The central columns are 25 feet 4 inches apart from centre to centre; the next pair 21 feet 7 inches; the next 17 feet 8 inches; and the outer 16 feet 3 inches, which is that of the flanks. He could not ascertain from any indication on the spot what the length of the temple was: but assuming it to have twenty pillars on the flanks, like that at Ephesus, it must have been 320 feet from angle to angle of the plinths of the outer columns. The pillars, as near as could be ascertained, were 60 feet in height, bearing an entablature of about 15 feet, and their capitals Mr. Cockerell remarks as "the most beautiful he had seen."[2] Besides its own intrinsic beauty, this capital is especially interesting here, as from the multiplied divisions of the lateral convolutions of the volutes it resembles the Persepolitan example more than any other example at present known. If the bases of the columns should happen to show an equal tendency to follow the principles of Persian design, it will be a step in advance in our history of the order which would be a great gain. It is not, however, so much in this great temple as among the minor ruins at Sardis that we can hope to trace back its history; but it is in this city, if anywhere, that we may expect to find the materials for this purpose. This, as well as the probable good preservation of the lower part of the great temple, makes us regret that it has not been excavated to a greater extent than has been done. It seems certainly to have been completed before the Persian wars, and may be as ancient as that at Samos. It certainly is older than either those of Ephesus or Didyme, as they now

exist, and though erected after the style had attained its complete form, might still afford some hints of the progress towards perfection.

Next to this in rank must be classed the temple of Diana Leucophryné at Magnesia, which is interesting from the details regarding it which Vitruvius quoted, apparently from a work written by its architect Hermogenes, of Alabanda.[3] At present, however, we are worse off for details of the construction than we are with reference to any of the other temples just named. It is completely ruined, apparently thrown down by an earthquake. It was partially examined in 1820 by a French architect, M. Huyot, in company with our countryman, Mr. Donaldson, and described by M. Raoul Rochette in a paper in the *Journal des Savans* in 1845.

[1] Temple of Jupiter at Agrigentum (Doric) . . . . 110 × 357 *
    Great Temple, Selinus (Doric) . . . . 165 × 330 †
    Temple of Juno, Samos (Ionic) . . . . 167 × 302 ‡
    Temple of Apollo, Didyme (Ionic) . . . . 163 × 364 §
    Temple of Diana, Ephesus (Ionic) . . . . 163 × 342 ‖
    Jupiter Olympius, Athens (Corinthian) . . . . 171 × 341 ¶
    If all these measurements were exact, some even of these slight discrepancies might disappear. They are all measured on the plan from the external angles of the plinths of the angle columns.

[2] All the particulars here detailed are derived from a paper by Professor Cockerell, contributed to Leake's *Researches in Asia Minor*, published by Murray in 1824, page 342 et seq.; it is, so far as I know, the only trustworthy source of information.

[3] Vitruvius, lib. iii. chap. 2.

* Cockerell in Stuart's *Ant. of Athens*, suppl. volume, pl. 1.   ‖ Himself, ibid., lot. & fr. Sards, pl. lviii.
‡ *Ant. of Ionia*, vol. 1 pl. lxiv.   † Gherr. *Bull. de Corresp. Hellenique*, p. 381 et seq.
§ *Ant. of Ionia*, pl. iii ch. 3.   Rayet et Thomas, *Gazette de Beaux Arts*, Juillet, 1876.
    Wood's *Discoveries at Ephesus*, p. 261.
¶ Stuart, *Ant. of Athens*, vol. iii. pl. ii. ch. 4.   Penrose, *True Principles*, pl. xxxviii.

From these sources we learn that, as mentioned by Vitruvius, it was pseudo-dipteral, and measured 100 feet across the front by 187 on the flanks. The columns appear to have been 41 feet 6 inches in height, having an entablature of 9 feet 6 inches in height.[1]

SMALLER IONIC TEMPLES IN ASIA.

There are two other temples in Asia Minor of the Ionic order, very similar in dimensions to the three illustrated in this volume, but apparently of more modern date. The first is that known as the temple of Jupiter, at Æzani;[2] it is pseudo-dipteral, and measures 72 by 121 feet, and the order, though still retaining considerable elegance, shows a tendency towards Roman forms. The architrave is exaggerated, the frieze is proportionately reduced, and ornamented with foliage in such a manner as to make it more like a part of the cornice than a distinct member, and the cornice itself is singularly insignificant. Practically the architrave forms one-half of the whole entablature, and that is only about one-fifth of the height of the columns. If it were not that it has so modern an appearance, probably belonging to the early times of Roman influence, one would be tempted to believe that its forms were copied from some Persian model, without going through the process of assimilation with the Doric order, which the more classical examples were subjected to. The fact, however, seems to have been that the Ionic order was never forced to submit to the same stern rules which governed design in the Doric order. While using it architects were allowed to play with principles in a manner most unusual in classical times. This may frequently have led to most pleasing varieties of forms, but, from this latitude, it is most dangerous to base any theories, either ethnological or chronological, on these peculiarities.

There is also an Ionic temple at Aphrodisias, in Caria.[3] It, too, is pseudo-dipteral, and measures 68 feet by 122. Its order—provided there is any authority for the parts above the architrave—is of a much more usual form than the last described, but the whole has even a more modern appearance. On each of the columns there are tablets containing inscriptions in Roman characters, but nothing that can be identified with any name or event that would enable us to fix the date of its erection. It would no doubt be interesting to determine this, because it is very curious to find these temples, though situated so far apart, almost identical in dimensions and disposition, though differing so far in date. Perhaps something more may be made out of these similarities and differences than has hitherto been done, when their peculiarities are studied with more care than even M. Texier was able to bestow upon them.

Besides these, there are three other temples of the Ionic order in Asia Minor which it is hardly necessary to allude to more in detail in this place, as they are illustrated further on and in fact form the substance of this volume. They are all very small when compared with the giants described above, and are smaller even than the two just mentioned. The largest of the three is that of Apollo Smintheus, in the Troad, which measures 74 feet by 132;[4] that at Priene measures 64 feet by 121, while the Temple of Bacchus at Teos is only 58 feet wide by 112 in length. That at Priene, however, makes up for the exiguity of its dimensions by a beauty of detail and elegance of proportion in which it is not surpassed by any Ionic temple of its class that we are acquainted with.

IONIC TEMPLES IN EUROPE.

Although, as hinted above (p. 2), no remains have been found in Europe of any peristyle temple of the Ionic order, there are three little shrines of such beauty that they cannot well be passed over. The largest, and perhaps also the oldest, of these, is one that once existed on the banks of the Ilissus near Athens, and was

---

[1] It is needless to inquire whether their dimensions are or are not rigidly correct, as the building was far more thoroughly explored by M. Texier during his expedition to Asia Minor in 1843. Nothing however was published by him in his report of that expedition,[*] apparently from a feeling of delicacy towards his assistant, M. Clerget, who really did the work of exploration and restoration, and who he consequently wished should reap the whole credit that was due to him. The results have consequently hitherto been inaccessible to the public, but are now in course of publication by MM. Bayet and Thomas[†]. As this memoir of M. Clerget will probably prove to be exhaustive, and contain all that is known or likely to be known about this temple, for the ruins are fast disappearing, it may be well, before speculating further regarding it, to await its appearance, which cannot now be long delayed.

[2] Texier, *L'Asie Mineure*, vol. i. pl. 21 to 33. See also Pullan and Texier, *Principal Ruins in Asia Minor*, pl. 10 to 16.

[3] Texier, *L'Asie Mineure*, vol. iii. pls. 151 to 154. Pullan and Texier, pls. 37 to 39.

[4] When we get full particulars regarding the Magnesian temple, they will be extremely interesting as affording means for comparison with that of Apollo Smintheus as illustrated in the present volume. The latter, it is true, is smaller, but like it is a pseudo-dipteral, and adorned with an I air of a singular elegance. It is doubtful however whether even this comparison, when it can be made, will enable us to ascertain the relative age of the two temples. The Ionic was used with such freedom and such absence of restraint, that neither the relative length of the columns nor the character of the details can be used as certain indices either of age or beauty.

[*] *Description de l'Asie Mineure*, three vols. folio, Paris, 1839-49.

[†] *Mémoire de la Grèce Asiatique*, by Bayet and Thomas, vol. i. p. 163.

described by Stuart in his first volume on the Antiquities of that city. It was tetrastyle and amphiprostyle, and notwithstanding this it measured only 40 feet 8 inches in length by 18 feet 7 inches across. The little temple of the Wingless Victory, in front of the Propylæa, was also amphiprostyle, but was even smaller, measuring only 16 by 24 feet but was a gem of beauty, and with its sculptured frieze, when perfect, must have been worthy of the situation where it was placed. It was erected apparently in 480 B.C. The third, that of Empedocles at Selinus, is of about the same dimensions (16 by 23 feet), but it has only four pillars in front, with a slightly recessed porch. If correctly ascribed to Empedocles it must be even more modern, as he died only in 444 B.C. Its most remarkable peculiarity is that the Ionic pillars of its façade are surmounted by a Doric entablature, with triglyphs and all the usual features of that order. So far as is known at present it is unique in that respect, but the arrangement may, in ancient times, have been more common. The whole efforts of the Ionian architects, in early ages, were directed to an attempt to elaborate out of the Assyrian style an order which would assimilate, without discord, with their own original Doric, and during the process it would be strange if they did not sometimes lean a little too much to one side or the other and mix up features which afterwards became quite incompatible.

ERECHTHEUM.

By far the most important, as well as interesting, example of the Ionic order in Europe is the double temple in the Acropolis at Athens, known as the house of Erechtheus.[1] Yet even it is not large (73 by 38 feet) without the northern and southern porches; but it is unsurpassed for elegance of detail and for appropriateness of design. Though the purposes to which the various parts were applied were numerous and diverse, every part is made to tell its own tale with a distinctness hardly to be found in any edifice of its class in any part of the world; still the whole are so blended together as to form a beautiful and harmonious group, without any incongruity in any part.

It seems impossible now to ascertain how much of the irregularity of its design arose from its having been erected on the lines of the original house of Erechtheus, which was burnt by the Persians. Nor do any remains exist which would enable us to say whether the original house was in the Doric or Ionic style; most probably the latter; and it may also have been partially in wood, as its being so would account for certain peculiarities in its design which are not otherwise easily explained. Be this as it may, what really interests the student of architecture most in this temple is, that it contains two, probably three, examples of the Ionic order, differing in detail and in proportions, but not to such an extent as to be incongruous, while it is difficult to say which is the most beautiful. None of them have ever been surpassed.

The pillars of the northern portico are nine diameters in height, and have bases more elaborately enriched than any others known, unless we may now except the six central ones of the principal front at Didymæ; but some of these last, especially those with twelve sides, though very rich, are of very questionable taste. Like all the pillars of this temple, those of the northern portico have the beautiful honeysuckle band or necking below the volutes which is peculiar to this temple, not being found elsewhere; and the volutes themselves are more elaborate and more beautiful than any other known examples. The pillars of the eastern portico are nine and a half diameters in height, and are simpler in all their details. Those of the west front were apparently of the same proportions as those of the eastern portico, but varied in detail, though what the difference was it is difficult now to say, as they have perished entirely, and were not drawn with sufficient care while still in situ. This little temple is in consequence a most instructive example of the freedom, it may almost be said playfulness, with which the Greeks could treat the designs of their temples when using the Ionic order, and not aiming at simple grandeur, which seems to have been the ruling idea aimed at in the erection of the neighbouring Parthenon.

The truth of the matter seems to be that the Greeks in Europe never considered the Ionic order sufficiently severe and monumental to be used as an external ornament for their temples, but as an internal order they used it extensively and with the best effect. Nothing can be happier than the mode on which it is introduced in the Propylæa, at Athens and Eleusis, where it is seen combined with the Doric forms of the exterior, and where each is employed exactly in the manner to which it was best suited. The same too was probably the effect in the Temple of Minerva at Tegea. In the Temple of Apollo at Bassæ it is so employed with the happiest effect, and may have been so in other places now too completely destroyed for its presence to be detected.

It was employed in the Parthenon, as there seems no doubt that the roof of the opisthodomos was supported by four columns of the Ionic order, probably of the same tall proportions as those of the Propylæa, or ten diameters in height.[2] This being the case, we cannot but wonder why they were not also introduced into the

[1] Ὄλυμπα Ἐρέχθειος ἐσιόθμενος. Pausanias, Bk. i. ch. 26.   [2] Penrose, Principles of Athenian Architecture, pl. 34.

cells, as at Rossæ, where their elegant and slender proportions were so much more appropriate than the heavier and thicker Doric shafts which we know were employed. It raises a strong presumption in favour of there having been galleries in those temples in which we find an upper tier of Doric pillars standing on the level of a lower range, as at Ægina and Pæstum, as well as in the Parthenon. Without the presence of some such direct utilitarian necessity, it is difficult to understand why the Greeks should ever have adopted an expedient which, judged of by their own principles, never could have been æsthetically beautiful. At the same time it is almost as difficult to see how the galleries could have been supported by the architraves at Pæstum and Ægina without arrangements, of which there is no evidence. But perhaps if these temples were now more carefully examined with reference to this purpose even this difficulty might be removed.[1] As there are no actual remains, now existing, of the internal order of the Parthenon, the question whether there were internal galleries, or not, must be determined from evidence derived from other temples. As it at present stands the evidence seems to be in favour of their existence there as well as in some other temples at least.

MAUSOLEUM AND TROPHY TOMB.

One of the most remarkable applications of the Ionic order to any building, was the mode in which it was employed to adorn the Mausoleum at Halicarnassus. This was considered so successful by the ancients that they raised the building, like the temple at Ephesus, to the rank of one of the Seven Wonders of the world;[2] though now that, thanks to the zeal and energy of Mr. Newton, we know very nearly indeed what its form and appearance must have been, we are at a loss to understand why it was so much admired when it stood entire.

The principal architectural ornament of the monument was a pteron of thirty-six Ionic columns of more than usual stoutness, being only eight and one-third of their diameters in height.[3] They measured consequently 28 feet 7 inches, and supported an entablature of more than usual heaviness, being 8 feet 9 inches in height, or three and one-third of that of the columns. These unusual dimensions were no doubt designed, and most skilfully so, to give adequate support to the pyramidal roof they were destined to carry. This pyramid, with the pedestal or meta on its summit, which carried the chariot of Mausolus, measured, like the pteron, 37 feet 6 inches in height. The order consequently was only about half the dimensions of that used at Ephesus, and, as every part of it is represented in the fragments in the British Museum, we are enabled to say it was in no respect more admirable. The " wonder " of the monument most consequently have resided, as at Ephesus, in the podium or stylobate on which it was raised. This from the dimensions quoted by Pliny could only have been about 34 to 34 feet in height, and, as its girth or circumference according to the same author was 411 feet,[4] its dimensions hardly exceeded those of an ordinary English parish church. It is true the markings in the rock show that this last dimension may have extended to 400 feet, or nearly so, for the outside of the lowest step; but this hardly adds to the general bulk of the base. This being so, it can only be owing to the mode in which this podium was treated architecturally, and the beauty and disposition of its sculptural ornaments, that this tomb, like the temple at Ephesus, from the same cause, could have excited such extraordinary admiration in the ancient world. It is this, however, and this only, that makes it difficult to restore the Mausoleum with almost perfect certainty. No fragments of architectural details which did not belong to the ordinary type of the Ionic order were found in the excavations, and nothing that seemed especially appropriate to the basement. Portions of the only frieze that could have belonged to it are in the British Museum, and the statues found on the spot, and the lions, though beautiful, of course, are not exceptionally so, and present no features to excite wonder. If it was, as has been suggested, that the Monte Cavallo Horses, now at Rome, really once adorned one angle of this base, and that three similar groups were placed at the three other angles, it would go far to remove our doubts. It may also be that twenty statues of the very highest class of Greek sculpture stood on the pedestals between the angles, and

<hr/>

[1] Pausanias' description of the Temple of Jupiter at Olympia, though not very distinct, seems certainly to indicate that there was such a gallery in that temple. Ἄνωθι δὲ χίονες δὶ καὶ ὅσαι τοῦ ἀναὰ κίονες καὶ ἐπαὰ τὸ ὑπὲρ ὑπερώον, καὶ πρόσοδος δὲ διὰ τῶν κιόνων καὶ τὸ ὑπερώον ἐστὶ ἀναβάσις (Eli. v. ch. 10). The term ὑπερώον can hardly apply to anything on the same level as the entrance, and must mean a gallery or upper chamber of some sort, and the winding stair that led to the roof could only be wanted in the event of there being a clerestory to which access was indispensable to adjust the curtains or blinds which may have been necessary to keep out the weather, where glass or some transparent substance was not employed. It certainly was not intended for the use of crowds or persons to get outside to repair the roof; but, like the stairs found in most of the Sicilian temples, meant continuous access by the priests or servants of the temple.

[2] It is curious that one out of the Seven Wonders of the world should belong to the Ionic order. No building in either the Doric or Corinthian style seems to have been considered worthy of that rank.

[3] Mr. Pullan, first a most careful examination of the dimensions of twenty-six columns measured by Mr. Newton at Halicarnassus and of these that are in the Museum, came to the conclusion, from the extent, that the pillars were 8½ diameters in height, and consequently within a small fraction either way of 29 feet 8 inches in height. The conclusion is complete in the Museum, as is drawn to a tenth scale by Mr. Pullan; see plate with its Mr. Newton's first work on Halicarnassus.

[4] Pliny, Hist. Nat. xxxvi. 5, which is the only written authority for the dimensions above quoted.

that there may have been removed by Imperial Roman soldiers, long before the decay of the monument. But unless something of this sort did occur we must be allowed to hesitate before admitting that this building, though no doubt very beautiful in itself, was entitled to rank as one of the seven most remarkable monuments of the ancient world.'

A very beautiful copy on a small scale of the Mausoleum,—if in fact it is not the original,—was found at Xanthus by Sir Charles Fellows in 1838, and all its architectural and sculptured features were removed by him and are now in the British Museum. In conjunction with Mr. Rhode Hawkins, who assisted him in the removal, he prepared a model on the scale of one inch to a foot, of the mode in which he supposed the building was originally arranged. This, however, cannot be said to be a satisfactory attempt at restoration. A better one was made by Mr. Falkener and published by him in the *Museum of Classical Antiquities*, vol. i. p. 236, *et seq.* Even it, though certainly nearer the mark, cannot be said to have solved all the difficulties of the problem.' It suffices, however, to convey a very fair idea of what this building was when complete. Its dimensions were very small, only 22 feet by 34 at the base, and about 40 feet in height. It consisted of a plain solid podium, adorned apparently by two lines of sculpture, and supporting a small Ionic temple of sixteen or twenty columns, each only nine feet in height. The order had no architrave, but a sculptured frieze of great beauty, and statues of very considerable elegance stood between the pillars.

The most disappointing matter in connexion with this little gem is, that, though so evidently a counterpart of the general design of the Mausoleum, it throws no new light on the construction of that more celebrated building. The same would be true if we assume that it is the model which suggested the design of the Mausoleum instead of a copy of it, which, from the style of its sculptures and other indications, seems to be most probably the case. Recent authorities indeed, suppose it to have been erected in the first half of the fourth century B.C. in honour of a native satrap or ruler of Lycia, probably the satrap Pericles, who, as we learn from a fragment of Theopompus, attacked and captured the town of Telmessus.' If, however, we were to trust to its teaching, we should restore the podium at Halicarnassus as a solid mass, without any architectural features, and only two friezes let into it, without any framing or any obvious connexion with the design which is almost impossible. If, however, the upper parts were satisfactorily restored, it might be useful in confirming, even if it did not suggest, any arrangement that might be suitable for the larger building.

It is much to be regretted that a few more buildings of abnormal design, like the Mausoleum and the Erechtheum, have not come down to modern times, inasmuch as if that had been the case they would have conveyed a very different idea of the principles of Grecian design from that generally prevalent. It has frequently been urged, as a reproach, that Greek temples are all alike, and that if you have seen one side of one of them, you have seen the other three. To those who are not sufficiently initiated in the delicate gradations, which form the especial charm of the style, this may to a certain extent appear true, but, to those who are familiar with its peculiarities, these apparently small differences are recognised as effecting marked diversity of graceful or dignified expression, and afford far more pleasure than the rude contrasts by which the mediaeval architects forced their varieties on the attention of the vulgar. Even then if the reproach could be admitted it applies to the Doric style only. The Ionic order was treated with far more freedom by the Greeks, and the Erechtheum, at Athens, and the Mausoleum, coupled with the smaller tombs and temples found everywhere, show that when they chose they could use contrasts with as much facility and grace as was at all desirable. The Doric was, in fact, the sacred order of the Greeks, and the forms of the temples to which it was chiefly applied were sanctified by long use, as much as any part of their liturgy or religious observances. The Ionic never—in Greece at least—attained to that eminence, and was used as the taste or caprice of the architect might dictate. This, however, with a people so artistic as the Greeks always were, both at home and in their colonies, led to such happy results that a few more examples would be a boon, the value of which, from an artistic point of view, it would be difficult to over-estimate.

' In 1862 I published a restoration of the Mausoleum, in which I attempted to combine the discoveries of Mr. Newton with the accounts of Pliny and of a curious reveal of its final destruction by the Knights of St. John in 1402. With regard to the upper part of the monument I have seen nothing to alter. The pyramid with its roots supporting the chariot seem quite certain, so too does the plinth; but below that the details of the podium do not admit of equal certainty. No architectural details were found that seem certainly to belong to it; and though its dimensions are nearly certain, it is still open to anyone to show how it could be made more worthy of its reputation.

' Anxious to see, nothing in the Museum could now to Mr. Falkener's restoration is there any suggestion of a doorway to the basement, but that such existed is nearly certain. In all the attempts at restoration I have seen the only means of access to the upper temple but adjoining even so a pair would have been by a ladder outside, which is nearly impossible. It is curious it never occurred to any one that the two missing slabs of the base frieze are missing because their place was occupied by a doorway 8 feet in width, over the monk step. Its position would be no difficulty, inasmuch as a building at Mylasa, which is also an exact copy of the Mausoleum, though of the Corinthian order and much later date, has its doorway on one side, and considerably out of the centre of the face, in which it is placed. The doorway too in the west front of the Erechtheum is quite unsymmetrical, being not of the centre and under one of the pillars of the portico above it.

' *Fragmenta Historicorum Graecorum*, Müller, Paris 1841, vol. i. p. 295.

CORINTHIAN ORDER.

It is hardly necessary, in a brief introductory essay like the present, to say much regarding the origin of the Corinthian order. It was hardly, if ever, used by the Greeks as a temple order, though no doubt invented by them. In such little gems as the so-called Tower of the Winds, and the Choragic monument of Lysicrates, it was used with a grace that was never surpassed, but in these instances it is more on the scale adopted by a carver in wood or marble for ornamental purposes, than of architecture properly so-called. There was also at least one Corinthian capital in the Temple of Apollo at Didyme,[1] which is unsurpassed for elegance by any afterwards employed, and another at Bassæ,[2] which may have been beautiful also, but is too much ruined for its design to be well made out. It is also nearly certain that a range of Corinthian pillars (probably ten or eleven) adorned the cella of the Temple of Minerva at Tegea, and with that small list we have exhausted nearly all we know of the employment of this order by the Greeks of the great age. It was afterwards, it is true, adopted by the Romans, and used, even on Greek soil, with a magnificence and richness before which the simpler Doric and more elegant Ionic must "pale their ineffectual fires," though, in spite of all its splendour, it never equalled them in all the higher qualities of architectural design.

The base and shaft of the order were borrowed, with very slight modifications, from those of the Ionic order previously in use, and so was the entablature in all essential parts, only very considerably enriched. It retained too, to the last, a reminiscence of its origin in the small angular volutes which support the angles of the abacus. It cannot, however, be said to have derived any feature from the pre-existing Doric, and remained throughout antagonistic to the principles on which that order was designed. The great essential feature which constituted the new order was the introduction of a tall bell-shaped capital, adorned with acanthus leaves. If we may apply to this feature the same logic that was used above, when trying to investigate the origin of the Doric shaft, we can hardly fail to admit that the idea of this capital was borrowed from Egypt. It is at all events certain that the Egyptians used tall bell-shaped capitals adorned with leaves of plants and other vegetable forms at least as early as the eighteenth dynasty, and therefore certainly before the twelfth century, B.C. It is true they only used the native papyrus, the lotus, and the palm branch, for the decoration of their capitals; this, however, was quite sufficient to suggest to an ingenious Greek how other vegetable forms might be applied to the same purpose, and once the acanthus was suggested it was found so pre-eminently appropriate for the purpose, that no other was employed down to the fall of the Roman Empire.

We have no certain knowledge of the time when the acanthus was first applied to the bell-shaped capital, nor who was the architect who first introduced it. It may have been Callimachus, though the silly story that Vitruvius adds to his account of the invention by him does much to discredit his title.[3] It certainly, however, was in his age, though more probably Scopas was the real inventor, from what we know of his career. Callimachus was more of a sculptor than an architect, and it must have required an architect of the most consummate genius and taste to apply so novel a form in such a manner that it was at once accepted by his countrymen, and its use preserved in with very little variation during the ensuing six or seven centuries. What makes this more remarkable is, that it was frequently adopted by peoples who had very little sympathy with the feelings of the Greeks and still less appreciation of the exquisite refinements of Grecian taste.

JAS. FERGUSSON.

[1] Ant. of Ionia, vol. I. ch. iii. pl. 8.   [2] Ant. of Athens, supplementary vol. pl. xx.
[3] Vitruvius, vol. iv. ch. I.

10. FRAGMENT OF A CAPITAL FROM THE TEMPLE OF ATHENE.[*]
Height 3 feet 10½ inches, Width 5 feet. In the British Museum. From a photograph.

CHAPTER I.

HISTORY OF PRIENÈ.

Among the most valuable results of the mission of Sir William Gell[*], in 1812, to the west coast of Asia Minor was his survey of the plain of the Mæander, which showed for the first time the true outline of the ancient coast, and corrected the errors of previous geographers.[*]

This survey shows that the arm of the sea known to the ancients as the Gulf of Latmos has been almost entirely filled up by alluvial deposit from the river Mæander, all that now remains of the Latmic Gulf being a small salt lake south of the present course of the river. The original coast line may be traced by the cities which were anciently ports on the gulf, and which Strabo describes in the following order; Miletos (now Palatscha), Herakleia (Baffi), Pyrrha, Myus, Priené (Samsun). The sites of Miletos, Herakleia, and Priené have been identified by extant ruins, those of Pyrrha and Myus have been approximately fixed by other evidence.[*]

Priené is situated at the foot of the lofty range of mountains north of the Mæander which was known to the ancients as Mount Mykalé, and is now called the Samsun Dagh. The natural features of the site are such as would have commended it to Greek maritime adventurers seeking to gain a settlement on the coast.

A rock so steep as to form a natural citadel, and of which the height is calculated by Mr. Pullan at a thousand feet, rises abruptly above lower rocky ground, which descending gradually to what was once the shore afforded room for the construction of spacious terraces and platforms suitable for Greek architecture.

At the foot of this city must have been the port, the exact position and dimensions of which cannot now be discerned.

It was probably inferior in size to the ports of Miletos and Myus, and though sheltered from the north by the lofty range of Mykalé could hardly have been sufficiently protected from the fierce gales so constantly blowing from the south on this coast. This is probably the reason why we find no mention of the use of this port in any of the naval operations which took place in the Latmic Gulf.[*]

Of the early history of Priené very little is known. Here, as at Ephesos and other parts of the same coast, the leaders of the Ionian migration[*] found the Karians established, and must have had to win territory from them by degrees; first getting a footing on positions of natural strength commanding harbours. Aipytos, son of Neleus, one of the leaders of the Ionian migration, is said to have founded Priené, which subsequently received

---

[*] The core of the volute is sunk, probably for the reception of a bronze ornament. I see no reason for doubting that a fillet of the same metal, whatever it was, was placed above the ogee ornament of this capital. The sinking above it, is only rough hewn as shown in the woodcut and could never, it appears to me, have been intended to be left in its present unfinished state.—J. F.

[*] *Antiquities of Ionia (Soc. Dil.)* 1821, part i. ch. 1, pl. i. pp. 14-19 ; Rayet et Thomas, *Milet et le Golfe Latmique*, pl. I. II.

[*] Rayet, *ibid.* Texte, i. pp. 30, 33.

[*] According to Scylax, *Periplus*, 97, Priené had two harbours, of which was a closed harbour, doubtless, for ships of war. Rayet remarks, *Milet*, p. 26, that Thucydides (viii. *passim*) while recording the successive movements of the Athenian and Lacedæmonian fleets in the gulf of Latmos, never once mentions the port of Priené, and thence concludes that it was already blocked up by alluvial deposit ; but it may also have been then reputed a "statio malefida carinis."

[*] Herodot. i. 142.

a second colony from Thebes, led by Philotas; hence this city was sometimes called Kadmê.[1] Shortly after the foundation of Ephesos by Androklos, son of Kodros, he is said to have come to the assistance of the Prienians, then attacked by the Karians. The victory was gained by the Ionian forces, but Androklos fell on the field of battle.[1]

The Ionic migration is supposed to have taken place late in the eleventh or early in the tenth century B.C., but no positive date can be fixed, and there were probably a succession of migrations. It is probable that the league of twelve Ionian cities was originally formed for the purpose of common defence against the Karians.

These twelve cities were, on the coast, Phokæa, Ephesos, Kolophon, Klazomenæ, Lebedos, Teos, Erythræ, Priené, Myus, Miletos, and the two island cities, Chios and Samos. These confederate states met at the temple of Poseidon Helikonios, on the promontory of Mykalê, to celebrate a festival at which, according to Strabo,[1] the Prienians, in whose territory the temple was, presided at the sacrifices. It is, probably, on account of this worship that we find the Neptunian trident a constant type on the coins of Priené, on which it is associated with the type of Athenê on the obverse.

The political importance of this league seems to have declined as the power of the Lydian dynasty grew. These kings made a series of expeditions against single cities of the Ionian league. Gyges took Kolophon, and made an inroad on Miletos and Smyrna; his successor, Ardys, took Priené, and continued the war against Miletos, which, after sustaining a siege of eleven years under his successors, Sadyattes and Alyattes, was finally subdued, together with all the other cities of Ionia, by Croesus, and, after his defeat by Cyrus, B.C. 546, submitted to the Persian rule after some resistance, in the course of which Priené was taken by Mazares and its inhabitants, according to Herodotus, sold as slaves.[1] It was probably not long before these events that the war took place between Priené and Samos which is mentioned by Plutarch in his *Quæstiones Græcæ*.[1] The subject of dispute was a territory on the mainland, opposite Samos. The Prienians, whose cause was supported by Lygdamis, tyrant of Naxos,[1] defeated the Samians, who abandoned the territory in dispute for a time, but about seven years later revived their claim, and, strengthened by an alliance with the Milesians, so utterly defeated the Prienians at a place called ἀρήν, that the expression ὁ παρὰ δρυὸς ὀλεθρος became a proverb to denote any signal calamity.

Peace seems to have been at length arranged between the two states through the mediation of Bias of Priené, who was one of the most celebrated statesmen of his time.[1] Though there is no direct evidence to that effect, it seems probable that the arrangement then entered into was afterwards broken through by Polykrates, tyrant of Samos, who entertained the design of conquering all Ionia, and who seems to have been at war with Miletos about B.C. 529-525.[1]

Priené joined in the Ionian revolt B.C. 499, and contributed twelve ships at the battle of Ladé, a contingent small as compared with the eighty ships furnished by the Milesians on the same occasion. After the fall of Miletos, B.C. 494, Priené, with the rest of the Ionian cities, must have again passed under the Persian rule. Whether the statement of Pausanias[1] as to the oppression of the Prienians by Tabalos the Persian, or subsequently by one of their own citizens, Hiero, refers to this period, or to some time before the Ionian revolt, we have no means of ascertaining. The next notice we have of Priené is the statement of Thucydides, that about B.C. 440 war broke out between Samos and Miletos concerning Priené.[1] The cause of this war was probably an attempt on the part of the Samians to recover the territory on the mainland, the possession of which had already, in the previous century, been a matter of contention. Why the Milesians, who formerly aided the Samians in attacking Priené, now changed sides, we have no means of knowing. It was the policy of Athens at this time to reduce all the islands to the condition of tributaries, and their jealousy of the maritime power of Samos led them to intervene in favour of Miletos. An expedition of nearly 200 ships, under Perikles, besieged Samos by sea and land, and reduced it to the condition of a tributary B.C. 439.

We may presume that after the reduction of Samos the Prienians were strong enough, with the aid of Athens, to expel their adversaries from the mainland. Priené appears in the list of Ionian tributaries of Athens, Olymp. 88, 4, B.C. 425.[1]

This is all that we know from history of the disputes between Samos and Priené as to the territory in question, but a long series of inscriptions enables us to follow the history of this dispute century by century down to the Augustan Age.

[1] Strabo, xiv. p. 633; Pausan. vii. 2, § 7; Evans, ad Dionys. Hac. 825; Diog. Laert. i. 5, § 8

[1] Pausan. vii. 2, § 6.   [1] Strabo, xiv. p. 639, and viii. p. 384.

[1] Herodot. i. 15, 142, 161, 162. Grote, iv. p. 273, remarks that the Prienians, who were the first assailed by Mazares, had perhaps been especially forward in the attack made by Paktyas on Sardis.

[1] Plutarch, Quæst. Græc. xx.   [1] Boeckh, Corpus Inscript. 2,254, l. 16.

[1] Boeckh, 2id 2,254, l. 22; Plutarch, Quæst. Græc. xx.   [1] Herodot. iii. 39.

[1] Pausan. vii. 2, § 7. If we could be sure that the Tabalos of Pausanias is identical with the Tabalos made governor of Sardis by Cyrus (Herod. i. 154), the rule at Priené would probably have commenced not long after the capture of the city by Mazares.

[1] Thucyd. i. 115.   [1] Kohler, Urkunden z. Geschichte d. Delisch-Attischen Bundes, pp. 77, 190.

These inscriptions, with one exception, were all found on the site of the temple of Athené Polias at Prienê, where two of them were copied by Chandler during his mission to Ionia and were afterwards published by Böckh. Others belonging to the same series were subsequently copied by Lebas, and are published in his *Voyage Archéologique*, edited by M. Waddington.[11]

In the course of Mr. Pullan's excavations, many more fragments of the same text were discovered, and together with most of those previously copied were transported to England, and are now in the British Museum as stated in Mr. Pullan's Report. The original text of this series of inscriptions was engraved on the wall-stones of the cella and on one of the antæ. The examination of the marbles and their arrangement according to their original sequence has involved much time and study. Mr. E. L. Hicks, to whom the work of editing these inscriptions has been confided by the Trustees of the British Museum, has now nearly completed his task, and the result of his labours will shortly be published in Part 3 of the *Corpus of Greek Inscriptions in the British Museum* now in the press. In the following account of the controversy between Samos and Prienê I have had the advantage of studying the unedited portions of the text as arranged by Mr. Hicks in combination with the parts previously published, and have largely profited by his commentary.

The territory in question, as we learn from these inscriptions, comprised several small districts called Batinetus, Dryussa, and a fort called Karion. Karion and Dryussa originally belonged to the people of Melia, a town in Karia, which appears, at some period unknown, to have been conquered and its territory divided among neighbouring states. According to the Prienians, Karion and Dryussa were then allotted to Prienê, an assertion which the Samians distinctly contradicted. Both parties cited the evidence of historians in support of their claim.

One of the most interesting inscriptions brought from Prienê after Mr. Pullan's expedition is the dedication of the temple of Athené Polias by Alexander the Great.[12] It is to be inferred from this dedication that the temple was at that time complete, or nearly so.

33. DEDICATION OF THE TEMPLE OF ATHENÉ POLIAS BY ALEXANDER THE GREAT.
Height 1 foot 7½ inches, Width 4 feet.

Another fragmentary inscription[13] seems to relate to some remission of tribute granted to the Prienians by the same monarch. It is to be inferred from these two documents that he did not favour the Samians in their claim to the territory then held by the Prienians. A passing mention of Alexander in one of the unpublished fragments seems to indicate that some settlement of the dispute was made by him. But not long after his death it revived, and, according to the usual habit of Greek cities at that time, an appeal was made to the most powerful of the successors of Alexander in turn. We learn from one of the inscriptions as yet unpublished that the first of these appeals was to Antigonus. This must have taken place between B.C. 306 and the death of that king B.C. 301. What his award was is only imperfectly recorded in a fragmentary inscription; its purport, however, seems to have been that matters were to be left as they had been settled by Alexander.

From this time onwards we have in the inscriptions evidence of a succession of awards. The first of these is the result of an appeal of both parties to Rhodes, to arbitrate between them as an ἔκκλητος πόλις.

The latter portion of this award is given in an inscription published by Böckh and Lebas,[14] of which the earlier part is still unedited; but the two together do not nearly make up the original text. We learn from this document that, at the joint request of the Samians and Prienians, the Rhodians appointed certain commissioners, who heard the pleadings of delegates of both parties in the temple of Dionysus at Rhodes, and in the Artemision at Ephesus. The commissioners also visited the territory and the fort called Karion, which were the subject of dispute. The pleadings of the Samians are unfortunately wanting, but the part of the pleading of their adversaries which has been preserved gives us interesting glimpses into the previous history of Prienê. The

[11] Böckh, *Corpus Inscr.* Nos. 2,905, 2,914. Waddington-Lebas, pl. v. § 4, Nos. 189-207.
[12] Böckh, *Corpus Inscr.* 2,904. Waddington-Lebas, No. 147.   [13] Waddington-Lebas, No. 188.
[14] Böckh, *Corpus*, 2,905, n. 3. Waddington-Lebas, No. 189.

delegates of Prienè allege that at a certain date, when Molpuros held the office of Stephanephoros, certain citizens fled into the fort of Karion to escape from the oppression of a certain τύραννος, then ruler of their city. They remained in this fort three years, in the course of which they made an appeal for aid to the Rhodians and, it would seem, to other Greek cities. It was probably through Rhodian intervention that they were enabled to return to Prienè after three years of exile. The date of these events is approximately fixed by Mr. Hicks to B.C. 304 to 301, mainly on the ground that the inscriptions allude to decrees addressed by the Prienians to Lysimachos and Demetrios, at this date. The remainder of the extant text gives the judgment of the Rhodians, confirming the Prienians in the possession of Karion and the territory about it. The date of this award is placed by Mr. Hicks B.C. 299, a time when the power and influence of Rhodes must have been great, in consequence of their successful defence when besieged by Demetrios B.C. 304.

This Rhodian award did not, however, satisfy the Prienians, and we find that they laid claim to the district called Batinetos, then in the possession of the Samians. The dispute, by mutual agreement, was referred to Lysimachos; his award is given in an inscription found at Samos and now at Oxford." In this inscription the king communicates to the Samians the unwelcome information that the evidence which had been submitted to him fully sustained the claim of the Prienians. The date of this royal letter would, according to Mr. Hicks be B.C. 287. No copy of it was discovered at Prienè, but it is fully confirmed by two documents—a decree of the Prienians bestowing honours on the king, and his reply to their embassy. The gratitude of the Prienians for so favourable an award expressed itself in the substantial form of a gold crown of the value of a thousand staters, a bronze statue, and a solemn yearly festival. In the king's reply, which is in a very fragmentary state, an allusion is made to an invasion of the Prienian territory by their neighbours the Magnesians. This attack probably took place shortly before B.C. 301, when the west coast of Asia Minor was assigned to Lysimachos after the battle of Ipsos.

The settlement effected by the mediation of Lysimachos did not last long. The Samians, who, as they allege in a subsequent pleading, had never really accepted the award of Lysimachos, but had lodged a protest against it at the time, revived their contention at some period between B.C. 261 and 246, when some adversity had befallen the Prienians, and referred the points at issue to Antiochos Theos, who appears to have decided in their favour; but we have no information as to this award except that, according to the assertion of the Prienians, Karion was not included in the claim urged by the Samians. The dispute still continued, and the next interference from without came from Ptolemy Euergetes, one of the most powerful princes of his time, who, according to the statement of the Prienians, sent a general called Antiochos to mediate between the two contending parties, with what result is not stated. About B.C. 200 the dispute revived. A second appeal was made to the arbitration of the Rhodians, whose award is partially preserved in a long but mutilated text, of which two main portions are published."

It appears from this document that the Samians disputed the justice of the former Rhodian award, and that both parties appealed to the testimony of certain ancient historians, the weight of whose authority seems to have inclined in favour of the Prienians, who further urged that their prescriptive title to Karion and Dryussa had been confirmed by several successive awards, and that they had exercised rights of possession which had not been challenged at the time by the Samians. After hearing the arguments on both sides, the Rhodians gave a second award which confirmed the Prienians in the possession of Karion and Dryussa," and added to this award a minute specification of the boundaries between the Samian and Prienian territory. After the defeat of Antiochos the Great by the two Scipios, the Consul Cn. Manlius was sent to Asia, in B.C. 189, to establish Roman authority, and in the following year, with the aid of ten commissioners sent to him by the Senate, he settled all pending questions as to the distribution of territory between the princes and cities." Among the claims he adjudicated on was the long-pending dispute between Samos and Prienè, which Manlius decided in favour of Samos. What followed the award of Manlius we learn from the Senatus Consultum, which comes next in the series of Prienian inscriptions." Both disputants sent envoys to Rome, where they pleaded face to face before the Senate. The result of this appeal was that the award of Manlius was set aside, and that of the Rhodians was confirmed. The date of this Senatus Consultum is B.C. 135. A revision of the landmarks by the Rhodians seems then to have been made by a joint commission of Samians and Prienians. Some fragments in Lebas," together with some smaller fragments as yet unpublished, seem to relate to this document.

Such is the history of this long protracted dispute between Samos and Prienè, which, beginning at least as early as B.C. 500, can be traced down at intervals through more than four centuries. Nor indeed can we be certain that the Senatus Consultum B.C. 135 finally settled this contention, for among the unpublished

" Bœkh, Corpus Inscr. No. 2,254.
" Ibid. No. 189-191, I. 90.
" Waddington-Lebas, Nos. 195-198.

" Waddington-Lebas, Nos. 190, 191, 192-194.
" Livy, xxxviii. 31. Polyb. xxii. 7.
" Ibid. Nos. 195-197.

fragments from Priene is one which is most probably part of an Imperial letter relating to the same subject. There were in antiquity many such disputes as to territory which were settled by the same mode of successive arbitrations, and the same final appeal to Rome. The history of some few of these may be traced by means of inscriptions. The inscription relating to the dispute between the two Cretan cities Hierapytna and Itanos,[a] and that recently discovered at Olympia, which gives the decision of the Milesians in regard to the long-standing contention between the Lacedaemonians and Messenians,[b] are documents well worthy to be studied in connection with the history of the dispute between Priene and Samos. Between the consulship of Manlius, B.C. 188, and the Senatus Consultum, B.C. 135, we find the Prienians involved in another difficulty, which forced them to appeal to Rome for protection. Ariarathes, surnamed Philopator, succeeded to the kingdom of Cappadocia, B.C. 163, but, a few years afterwards, was dethroned by a rival claimant of the throne, Orophernes, a suppositious child of the late king, who was supported by Demetrius Soter. Ariarathes fled to Rome B.C. 158, and appealed to the Senate, which restored him to his kingdom, though Orophernes seems to have been allowed some share of the government.[c] This joint sovereignty, however, did not last long, for Polybius speaks of Ariarathes as sole king about B.C. 154.[d] In his youth Orophernes had been bred up in Ionia, and it was probably in consequence of early associations that on his accession he deposited 400 talents with the Prienians as a resource in time of need.[e] On the restoration of Ariarathes to the throne he claimed from the Prienians the sum deposited by Orophernes. Having refused to give up this money the Prienians were involved in a war with Ariarathes and his ally Attalus, King of Pergamos, in which they suffered greatly, appealing for assistance to Rhodes, and afterwards to the Roman Senate. Ultimately they seem to have given back the 400 talents to Orophernes as the depositor of this treasure.[f] It was probably after his dethronement that Orophernes conspired with the people of Antioch against Demetrius, King of Syria, who had been his benefactor. His conspiracy having been detected he was thrown into prison by Demetrius, who spared his life because it suited the policy of that king to maintain the pretensions of a rival to the throne of Cappadocia as a menace to Ariarathes.[g] The statements of ancient historians about this deposit are singularly confirmed by two unpublished fragments of inscriptions found on the site of the temple of Athené Polias, in one of which there seems to be a reference to the treasure of Orophernes as having been deposited in the temple of that Goddess, and the kings Ariarathes and Attalus are both mentioned; and even without this evidence it would have been a priori probable that such would have been the case, for the Greek temples were, as is well known, constantly used as banks of deposit. But this assumption is confirmed by a very curious discovery which took place after the expedition sent by the Society of Dilettanti had finally abandoned the site of the temple.

When Mr. Pullan cleared away the ruins which encumbered and concealed the marble floor of the temple, he left undisturbed the lower courses of a large pedestal at the west end of the naos, which had been anciently separated from the pronaos by bronze gates the position of which was indicated by grooves in the pavement forming segments of circles.[h] We can hardly doubt that on this pedestal once stood the colossal statue of Athené, mentioned by Pausanias, of which an arm, hand, foot, and other fragments were found in the ruins and are now in the British Museum. In April, 1870, just a year after Mr. Pullan had left Priene, Mr. Clarke, of Sokói, visited the site of the temple, where he found a number of masons from the neighbouring Greek villages ruthlessly converting the beautiful marble into gravestones and chimney-pieces. The courses of the pedestal had all been removed except the four centre stones of the lowest course. The discovery which Mr. Clarke then made is thus recorded by him in a letter which I reprint here from the *Numismatic Chronicle*, where it originally appeared:—

"Marshall's Hotel, Cavendish Square, W.
"9th December, 1870.

"MY DEAR SIR,

"I have received your note of the 7th inst., and willingly supply you with the particulars of how I found the Orophernes coins, olive-leaves, ring, and terra-cotta seal. They are as under.

"My wife, niece, and self paid a visit of inspection to Priene, just one year since we dined there with Messrs. Newton and Pullan. These gentlemen then kindly gave me all particulars about the temple, and showed me the pedestal where the statue of Minerva was supposed to have stood. This consisted of a large base, composed of many large stones of about six hundredweight each. It was then in proper order. On the occasion of my last visit (in April 1870) I found all these stones disturbed from their places, excepting four in the centre of the pedestal. This destruction was apparent to me immediately on my entry to the cella; and

[a] Boeckh, *Corpus Inser.* No. 2,561 b, Addenda, p. 1104.   [b] *Archäol. Zeitung,* Berlin, 1876, pp. 128–139.
[c] Diodor. xxxi. (*Eklo. iii.* p. 517), ed. Bipont, n. p. 25; Polyb. xxxi. 3; Xenophon, *Anab. lv. 26,* p. 1609 f.
[d] Polyb. xxxii. 12; Livy, *Epit.* xlvii.; Clinton, *Fast. Hell. iii.* p. 436.
[e] Diodor. xxxi. (*Excerpt. de Virt. iii.* p. 580), ed. Bipont, n. p. 41; Athen. n. p. 440.
[f] Polyb. xxxiii. 4.   [g] *Justin,* xxxv. 1.
[h] See Mr. Pullan's *Report, post,* p. 99, and pl. vi.

while standing in the midst of these tumbledown stones, lamenting the mischief done, by chance I found at my feet a coin covered with dirt. I washed it, and found it to be silver, and read the name Orophernes.

"I then went in search of my wife and niece, who were in the treasury, to inform them of my good luck, and again returned to the base of Minerva's pedestal, when the idea struck me that something more might be found under the four intact stones already referred to, so I employed two Greek masons who were working amongst the ruins, trimming stones for graveyards. With the aid of three crowbars we moved the first stone, and found under it a silver coin, similar to the one previously picked up; under the second stone we found another coin similar to the previous two. I then called my wife and niece to assist me in my discovery. On their coming up, we removed the third stone, and found a part of a ring—say a garnet set in gold, and some crumbs of gold; under the fourth stone we found a gold olive-leaf, a terra-cotta seal, and some crumbs of gold. We searched amongst the rubbish for more, but without success, so went to lunch in the treasury.

"During lunch the two Greek masons, with two or three other Greeks from Kelebesch, who came to Priene, hearing I was there, to pay me a visit, as well as Yuruks from the hillside, who, seeing Franks excited at having found something, came down to the spot to join in the kismet. All commenced scratching in the most perfect harmony, wondering at my good kismet at having found so much in so short a time, and their bad kismet at not being able to find anything. This was on Saturday, so on Sunday the inhabitants of Kelebesch, having heard of the well-eared Franks' discovery, turned out, bound to Priene, in search of treasure, two Jews accompanying them with a fair supply of money to purchase any bargain that might turn up. A grand turning over of stones took place by this mob of men, women, and children, but nothing was found. However, on the Monday afterwards, the Greek masons found amongst the earth of Minerva's pedestal a gold olive-leaf and two coins similar to those found by me. I purchased the broken coin (now in your possession) and the olive-leaf of the masons. The other coin was sold to Mr. John Forbes, making in all five coins. I presented one to the British Museum, one to the Dilettanti Society, gave one to my wife, and one to my niece. My wife has the olive-leaves and seal, and my niece the ring.

"I remain, dear Sir,

"Yours very truly,

"To General Fox."　　　　　　　　　　　　　"A. O. CLARKE.

The six coins found under the pedestal were all silver, with the same type and legend, and may be thus described:"

12.　　　　　　　　　　　　13.

COIN OF OROPHERNES.

[Obv.] Male head to right, beardless, bound with a diadem. [Rev.] ΒΑΣΙΛΕΩΣ ΟΡΟΦΕΡΝΟΥ ΝΙΚΗΦΟΡΟΥ. Victory moving to left, clad in a tunic chiton and diploidion, holding in her right hand a wreath, in her left a palm branch, in front of her a serpent on an altar; below the altar, monogram.

The Victory on the reverse of these coins has an evident reference to the title ΝΙΚΗΦΟΡΟΥ, assumed by Orophernes in the legend. A pair of wings of bronze gilt, which probably belonged to a small statue of Victory, were found in the ruins of the temple. These coins, while they differ in type and fabric from the coinage of the other kings of Cappadocia, remind us in their general treatment of the contemporary coinages of Ionia and Æolis, and their weight is adjusted to the same late Attic standard, as the silver money of many cities and kings of Asia Minor. As Orophernes was bred up in Ionia it is probable that he would adopt the style of coinage in use there, and very possibly these tetradrachms were struck for him in the mint at Priene. In that case the owl on the reverse may be the mint-mark of Priene. Mr. Clarke stated to me that the three coins picked up by himself under the lowest course of the foundation stones were lying in small hollows prepared for them in the bed of the course. It seems impossible, therefore, to resist the conclusion that these coins, as well as the gold ornaments described in Mr. Clarke's letter, were deposited under the foundations of the temple when the statue was originally set up. The dedicator of the statue was therefore, probably, Orophernes himself. As the citizens of Priene suffered much heavy loss in his cause, he may have dedicated the statue in gratitude for their fidelity

[b] These coins are published in the Numismatic Chronicle, New Series, vol. xi. p. 18.

in refusing to give up the deposit committed to their charge. Whether the coins or any other objects found with them were deposited under the pedestal in commemoration of the dedicator, or as an offering to the goddess, as her due for the custody of the treasure, is a question on which we should be better able to form an opinion if we knew the exact position in which the other three coins mentioned in Mr. Clarke's letter were found, and, also, if we could be sure that no others were found, either before or after his visit. The custom of commemorating the laying a foundation stone by placing coins under it may have been not unknown to antiquity, but I have found no other recorded instance of such a practice, except in the case of a gold tablet inscribed with the name of Ptolemy Euergetes I., which is said to have been found in the foundation of a small temple at Canopus, in Egypt, placed between two vitreous tiles." The great excitement which Mr. Clarke's discovery at Priene produced in the neighbourhood led to the complete destruction of the pavement of the temple. Since that time the work of destruction has been constantly going on unchecked."

Such are the few facts relating to the history of Priene which can be gleaned from ancient authors or recent discoveries. In the course of Mr. Pullan's excavations, several very perfect inscriptions were found containing decrees in honour of Prieniuns, who had interposed their good offices in the settlement of disputes between the citizens of other states. Thus among the inscriptions discovered by Mr. Pullan we find decrees of the cities of Iasos, Erythrae, Laodicea and Lycetus, Alexandria Troas, and of an unknown Doric city, in honour of Prienian citizens who had acted as dikasts in trying lawsuits in those several cities. Another inscription seems to be the fragment of a treaty between Priene and Miletos to secure the due administration of justice in cases where one of the parties was a foreigner, so that a Prienian in a Milesian court, or a Milesian in a Prienian court, might be on the same footing as a native citizen. Such lawsuits were called by the ancients δίκαι ἀπὸ συμβόλων. Evidence of friendly relations between Athens and Priene is to be found in the fragments of two Athenian honorary decrees, the date of which, according to Köhler, would be after Olympiad 111, 2-3, B.C. 335-34, when Alexander released the Greek cities of Asia Minor from Persian rule."

After the Roman conquest of Asia Minor we find no more historical notices of Priene. Its harbour must have become useless before the date of Strabo, for he states that in his time the city was 40 stades, = 5 miles, distant from the sea." Whatever political importance it may have had must have disappeared when it ceased to be a port.

C. T. NEWTON.

" Boekh, Corpus Inscr. No. 4,694.
" Corpus Inscr. Attic. Berlin, 1877, ii. pt. 1. Nos. 165, 164.

" Bayer, Hist. ii. p. 3.
" Strabo, xiv. p. 579.

14. IONIC CAPITAL FROM ONE OF THE EXTERNAL COLUMNS OF THE PROPYLAEUM IN THE TEMENOS OF ATHENÉ POLIAS.
In the British Museum. From a photograph.
Length 2 feet 9½ inches. Height from the bottom of volute 1 foot 1½ inch. Width 2 feet.

On the top are two oblong sinkings with side channels for running lead into sockets of dowels.

Mr. PULLAN'S REPORT OF THE EXCAVATIONS AT PRIENÈ.

The firman authorizing excavations at Prienè which was sent to me by Lord Lyons in 1866 required renewal in 1869. Although I reached Smyrna on September 4th, the new vizirial letter was not forwarded from Constantinople until October 10. No time was lost, however, by the delay, as the recent rains had rendered the interior of the country, and especially the valley of the Mæander, so unhealthy that two-thirds of the inhabitants were attacked by fever of a severe type, which occasionally proved fatal. In these circumstances it would have been unadvisable to have commenced operations. I therefore waited in the neighbourhood of Smyrna until the great heat had moderated and the fever had subsided, which was the case about the third week in October.

During the interim I made preparations for the journey. I engaged the old and experienced dragoman Spiro, who had accompanied me on former expeditions, and also two Turkish corporals of militia to act as guards and to superintend the labourers in the excavations.

We left Smyrna on October 14 by the Aidin Railway, and proceeded as far as the Balhjik Station. Here we engaged horses and camels to carry us, and our tools and tackle, to Sokïi, a distance of four or five hours from the station. Our road lay through the ruins of the Temple of Diana Leucophryenè at Magnesia ad Mæandrum. The walls of the peribolus are standing to a height of about 30 feet, and within the inclosure and around the ruins of the temple there are still to be seen the trenches dug by the late M. Texier at the time of his exploration of this district. At Sokïi we took up our quarters in the house of our friend Mr. Clarke, who had entertained me when I made the preliminary survey for the Society of Dilettanti in the year 1861. On the following morning I presented my letter of authority (called by the Turks bayraldi) to the Kaïmakam of Sokïi. He expressed strong disapproval of my proposed plan of encamping on the Samsun Dagh, the mountain upon which stood the ancient city of Prienè. He had himself brought about the destruction of a band of Greek brigands who had infested the neighbouring hills, and who had only a few months previously wined and carried off the nephew of the Dutch consul at Smyrna; therefore he had reason to speak strongly on the subject. I was not, however, in a position to promise to take his advice, as it was of importance that our tents should be pitched as near as possible to the ruins of the temple.

On the 16th we rode to Prienè, a distance of about four hours. Our road lay along the northern side of the valley of the Mæander, which is here about six miles wide, perfectly level, and bounded on both sides by ranges of high mountains—by that of Mycale on the north and that of Latmos on the south.

Leaving the village of Kelebesh on the right, we ascended the hill upon which the ruins of Prienè are situated. I found the heap which marked the site of the Temple of Athenè Polias much in the same state that it was in 1861, except that a draped figure near the ruins had been broken in pieces.

Prienè is situated on a low spur of Mount Mycale, some two hundred feet above the level of the plain. It was surrounded by walls which can still be traced on all sides but the north, where a great precipice rises to a height of a thousand feet. In the higher part of the city, almost immediately under this precipice, there is a platform of rock bounded by terrace walls. Upon this platform stood the Temple. Here, and in the agora beneath it, are the only level spots of ground within the city walls. The remainder of the city was built on the side of the hill, and approached by flights of steps cut in the solid rock.[1] In order that I might have the works immediately under my eye, I decided to pitch the tents at the west end of the platform. We commenced operations as soon as the camels with tools arrived and the camp was formed.

The heap of ruins extended about 150 feet in length by about 100 in breadth, and was 15 or 16 feet in height at the highest point.[2] It consisted of drums of columns, wall-stones and architrave stones, heaped together in confused masses, and partly covered with earth, on which low bushes were growing. The platform being narrow, there was hardly room for a passage between the ruins and the natural precipice which formed the boundary on the north; and we were obliged, in order to clear the site, to throw many of the stones, after they had been measured, into the valley below.

By October 26 we had ascertained that the wall of the cella on the north side was standing to a height of 5 feet above the level of the pavement of the peristyle, and that this pavement and the steps beyond it were in situ. The plinths and bases of several columns were also discovered, many of them slightly moved from their original positions. As I found that the height of the wall on this side would preclude the removal of the stones which evidently filled the cella, I determined after a few days' work to attack the south side of the heap. Here we found a gap in the cella wall, and at the south-west angle were found stones of the capitals of antæ.

On November 1st there was a severe gale, from which our encampment, being in an exposed situation, suffered severely. A wooden hut, which I had erected for photographic purposes, was blown away bodily, and its contents

[1] See *Antiquities of Ionia*, 2nd edit., pt. i. and frontispiece, plate ii.
[2] See the view of these ruins, *Ibid.*, plate iii.

entered far and wide; consequently we were compelled to move the tents to gardens in the valley of the Mæander. Here fever, which had attacked the two Turks from Smyrna, developed itself to such an extent that they begged me to send them home lest they should die. At this time I received a despatch from Mr. Cumberbatch, H.B.M. Consul at Smyrna, enclosing a letter from Ismail Pacha, the governor of the province, urging me to leave the unsafe encampment on the mountain, and to go to the neighbouring village of Kelebesh, stating that, unless we did so, he would not be responsible for our safety any longer. As this could not be done without great inconvenience, I wrote in reply that we were no longer on the mountain, that we were well armed, and that we had several men within call.

On November 10th I had a sharp attack of fever and ague, and Spiro also being disabled in the same way, I determined to abandon the diggings for a time, leaving the tents and stores in charge of two of my head workmen, and sending Spiro to Smyrna. I had subsequently to return to Smyrna myself in order to engage another dragoman.

Before leaving Priené I selected the most perfect of the mediæval ruins on the site, and left instructions that it was to be rendered habitable for the winter.

On December 16th I returned to Priené, and resumed work on the south side. By means of the gap in the wall on that side we were enabled to remove the stones and earth from the interior. In a foot or two above the pavement of the cella the earth was of a black colour, probably from the decomposition of the wooden beams of the roof, or still more probably from the effects of a fire.

The pavement of the cella was found entire, and at the west end the foundation of a large pedestal was uncovered, adjoining the wall of the posticum.[1] Near this pedestal we found the foot of a colossal statue, and fragments of an arm of corresponding dimensions.[2] Behind the pedestal were found two bronze wings, apparently those of a Victory, which may have been associated with the colossal statue which once must have stood on the pedestal. Proceeding towards the east we found the wall between naos and posticum standing, also an architrave enriched with olive-leaves, marking the position of the great portal.

In the pavement were grooves forming segments of circles in which the two halves of the principal door had worked, also the sockets of a metal railing which crossed the naos in front of the statue. Three steps led from the posticum to the cella, and on the uppermost rise there was an inscription in Greek characters, but of Roman times. The pavement of the posticum was formed of slabs of marble almost square, and at the sides adjoining the walls there were ranges of pedestals upon which statues had been placed. Here were found fragments of a draped figure, a female head, and other remains of sculpture.[3]

The clearing out of the interior of the temple was somewhat laborious on account of the distance the stones had to be removed, and occupied us until the end of January. When this was accomplished I directed the workmen to the peristyle on the south side, and to the portico at the west end. Here I had the satisfaction of finding two columns of the posticum standing to a height of 10 feet above the pavement. Between these two columns the architrave of a doorway was standing: this doorway led to a chamber, possibly a treasury, which occupied the space between the columns and the cella wall. This treasury appears to have been protected by metal gratings fixed between the columns and the antæ. The steps of the

[1] See Plate v. xi, xv.
[2] See marked post, p. 51. Some of these fragments of sculpture evidently belong to the colossal statue of Athene Polias, which remains existing at Priene in her time, and which must have stood on the pedestal.
[3] Plate xviii, xx; also Kupfer of Thomas, Musée de Gods Antiques, pl. 15.

portion at the west end were in situ, and the plinths of the columns were also in position, but they were much damaged at the angles.[4]

On February 18th the men were transferred to the north side. At the south-east corner several stones, bearing inscriptions which had belonged to the naos or to cella walls, were discovered.

The early part of the month of March was very rainy, so that our work was interrupted for some days; but by the 8th we were enabled to commence the east end of the cella, which was the only part uncovered.

On the 20th of March I was informed by Mr. Clarke, of Sokói, that the Kaimakam had notified to him an order from the Porte to the effect that all excavations throughout the empire were to be suspended until further notice.

As at that period sufficient information for the completion of the plan had not been obtained, and as any delay would have necessitated the abandonment of the diggings till after the hot summer months, I determined to proceed with the work more vigorously than ever until stopped by an order from the British Consul in Smyrna, to whom alone I was responsible. By doubling the number of workmen I had by the 23rd of March completed the circuit of the temple, and made some progress towards the excavation of the temenos.

At this period I applied for a further grant for the removal of sculpture and inscriptions, and for the excavating of the Propylæa. While waiting for a reply, having completed the excavation of the temple itself, I discharged all my men but three or four, who were simply employed in moving stones.

On the 6th of April Mr. Newton arrived from England, bringing a further supply of funds, and an authorization from the Society of Dilettanti to proceed further with the excavations. About this time we received a warning from Mr. Cumberbatch, and also from Mr. Clarke, of Sokói, that a band of nineteen brigands had sailed from one of the Greek islands, and that it was supposed their destination was Priené. Taking all precautions against surprise, we expedited the work as much as possible, and had almost concluded operations when a canvas from the Kaimakam arrived with an order to imprison any one who worked for me. Fortunately Mr. Newton, who had heard of the order for the suspension of excavations when at Smyrna, had written to Mr H. Elliot on the subject, and a few hours after the arrival of the canvas an official message was received from Constantinople authorizing us to continue the operations.

By April 26 all the fragments of architecture, sculpture, and inscriptions which could be transported by horses or camels had been despatched to the care of Mr. Clarke, of Sokói. Ninety-one such cases were conveyed on horse-back and twenty on camel-back.

There remained a number of marbles too heavy to be thus transported. These were all marked and left in the charge of the dragoman of the expedition, to be conveyed in carts to Balfajik, the nearest station of the Smyrna and Aidin Railway, as soon as the summer heat had sufficiently hardened the plain of the Mæander to make it fit for the transport of heavy goods on wheels.

This was accomplished by the end of August, and the marbles were shipped on board H.M.S. Antelope in September, 1869, and arrived in London February, 1870.

The transport of these marbles to England did not form a part of the original scheme of Mr. Pullan's mission, nor had the Society of Dilettanti funds available for the cost of such operations, which amounted to about £400. This expenditure, however, was provided by the liberality of Mr. Ruskin, who had placed at Mr. Newton's disposal a sum to be employed in excavation on sites where remains of Greek art might be looked for, and who kindly per-

[4] See Plate xix, xxi, xxii.

mitted that a large portion of this sum should be spent at Priene. These marbles were subsequently presented to the British Museum by the Society of Dilettanti.]

REMARKS ON THE STYLE, WORKMANSHIP, THE MODE AND MATERIALS EMPLOYED IN THE CONSTRUCTION OF THE TEMPLE.

The Temple of Athena Polias at Priene is one of the few Greek buildings in Asia Minor the date of which can be fixed with anything like absolute certainty. A well-known inscription[1] on one of the antæ states that it was dedicated by Alexander the Great. This dedication must have taken place about fourteen or fifteen years after the erection of the Mausoleum.

The sculptured ornaments throughout the building, such as the honeysuckle pattern on the cymatium, are delicately carved and of excellent style. The temple was constructed of a bluish marble quarried in the neighbouring mountain. It is of fine grain and admits of a high polish. The capitals of the antæ and a sculptured frieze, of which only a few fragments were discovered, were of fine white marble. The masonry is of a superior character, the joints being so close that the eye hardly detects them in the courses still in position.

The temple was built upon a natural rocky platform bounded on the south and east sides by a retaining terrace wall of heavy masonry, constructed of the same material as the temple itself. All the work was put together with iron cramps, except the beams and fronts of the columns, which were united by means of copper dowels as in the case of the Mausoleum at Halicarnassus, an edifice of nearly contemporary date, and probably built by the same architect.

DATA FOR THE RESTORATION.

Three steps and a surrounding narrow ledge remain on all sides of the temple. This ledge is on a level with the pavement of the temenos, which extended to the east only; on the other sides there is simply the levelled rock.

The pavement of the peristyle was perfect all round, though at the angles it is a little shaken with the fall of the cella walls. Plinths of most of the columns, more or less broken, remain in situ; where they no longer exist, their position can be ascertained by slight sinkings in the surface of the pavement. None of the moulded bases remain in position and perfect with the exception of three of the columns of the posticum. In some cases the flutes on the upper side of the torus of the base were left undivided.

All the members of the order were found except the frieze. A few fragments of figures in relief were discovered, but there is no evidence that these formed part of the frieze of the order.

Parts of the bases and capitals of the antæ were recovered, but there were no mouldings found which afforded a clue to the mode in which the ceiling of the cella was constructed.

ARCHITRAVE.

This member was in two pieces; the outer stone had three fasciæ, and on the under side there was a sunk panel with an enriched border. The inner stone had two fasciæ, and was surmounted by an ovolo moulding. On the outer stone in place of a moulding there was a ledge, but the moulding which fitted into this ledge was found in various places in the vicinity of the architrave.

[1] See note, p. 22. *Antiquities of Ionia,* part i. Pl. iii. p. 12.
[2] See pl. xii. and the description of the Plate, p. 33.

This mode of carving the moulding on a separate stone was largely used in the Mausoleum, and there is an example of it in the Erechtheum.

CORNICE.

Above the frieze there was a bold ovolo, and above it a row of dentil stones, the whole being crowned by a corona and a cymatium, enriched with a bold honeysuckle ornament, and lions' heads at intervals.[1]

LACUNARIA.

Several stones both of the upper and lower lacunaria were dug up.

TRANSVERSE BEAMS.

Many of these were found; they had two fasciæ on each side, with sunk panels underneath, corresponding with those on the architraves.

TEMENOS.

The rocky platform on which the temple stood was of an oblong form. At its east end was a square area, measuring about 125 feet each way. West of this the platform narrowed suddenly, and on this narrower space the temple was built, at a distance of 60 feet from a retaining wall, which bounded the platform on the south side, but only 15 feet from the precipice which bounded it on the north.

The foundations of a Greek wall were to be traced on both sides running parallel to the temple and terminating opposite the steps at its east end.

To the east of these walls the boundary of the *temenos* on the north side seems to have been formed by a series of pedestals, and on the south and west sides by a low wall with seats at intervals.

Upon the terrace retaining wall to the south there seems to have been a Greek Doric colonnade. Pieces of the architrave and cornice of this colonnade were found both upon and below the platform.

Westward of the temple the platform of rock narrowed to about sixty feet and terminated in jagged rocks.[2]

PROPYLÆUM.

This edifice is built on the eastern boundary of the *temenos.*

It is constructed with stones from an earlier edifice, and appears to be of the Roman period; the pavement is formed of wall-stones, and the doorstep has an inscription of the Macedonian period built into it upside down.

This building was thoroughly excavated,[3] but no trace of the six piers in the interior as shown in the plan (Plate 11 of the *Antiquities of Ionia*) could be found.

ALTAR.

Between the east front of the temple and the Propylæum I laid bare the foundations of an oblong structure of Græco-Roman times. The upper and lower mouldings of a podium were found, but no stones which afforded data for the restoration of the upper part.

These remains are probably the basement of a great altar.[4]

[1] Plate ix. xxx.   [2] Plate ii. ii. v.
[3] See the plan, Plate v. Compare *Antiquities of Ionia,* part i. pl. 11, and the architrave details, ibid. pl. 12-13.
[4] See Plate v. These remains are not noticed in the description of the temenos in the *Antiquities of Ionia.*

NOTE.

At page 29 of his Report on the Excavations at Priene Mr. Pullan states that on the upper step leading from the pronaos to the naos there was a Roman inscription. From a note which I took at the time I find that this inscription was a dedication in Greek by Marcus Antonius Rocvicus, son of Marcus, of the three steps, τριβαθμός to Athene Polias and Augustus. The word τριβαθμός seems to be new: of its meaning there can be no doubt, as there are three steps, on the uppermost of which the inscription was found. While drawing up the memoir on Priene in this volume I had unfortunately mislaid this note, which I only came upon after my memoir had been printed off.　　　　　　　　　C. T. N.

FRAGMENTS OF SCULPTURE AND ARCHITECTURE

DISCOVERED IN THE TEMENOS OF ATHENÉ POLIAS AT PRIENÉ, AND NOW IN THE BRITISH MUSEUM.

16.

Female draped torso, the head to the base of the neck, both arms from above the elbow, the left foot and ankle, and nearly all the right foot wanting. The body is clad in a talaric chiton with sleeves, over which is a thicker chiton without sleeves, fastened on each shoulder; the waist is encircled with a flat girdle, perforated with holes at intervals for the reception of some metallic ornament. The figure, which has the slim proportions of a young girl, rests on the left leg, the right being slightly bent. The drapery is treated with a severe simplicity, which would make the statue suitable for forming part of an architectural design. The head and both arms have been attached by a joint a little above the elbow. The sculpture is probably of the same age as the temple, and executed in the same school as the sculpture of the Mausoleum. The surface of the marble is discoloured, as if from the action of fire. When found, this torso was broken into five fragments. Height, 4ft. 3in.

Left foot of colossal female figure, cut off by a joint about half way between the instep and the end of the toes. The marble is pierced between the great toe and the next toe, as if for the insertion of some metallic object. The base of the great and next toes and of the right side of the foot are cut away near the joint, showing that the heel of

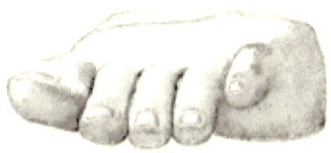

17.

the foot was raised. The upper part and left side of the foot are roughly tooled, and on this rough margin is a perforation opposite the space between the great and next toe. This rough margin is probably wrought for the reception of a bronze sandal. (Breadth 1ft. 2½in., length 1ft.) With this left foot were found the following fragments.

Fragment of a colossal left hand, broken off at the wrist, the fingers and upper joint of the thumb wanting; this is made up of many pieces. Breadth 1ft. 4½in., length 1ft. 8in.

A colossal left upper arm, made up of 69 fragments, which have been put together since the marbles from Prienè have been presented to the British Museum. Length 4ft. 2in., thickness 1ft. 7in.

All these fragments are more or less discoloured by the action of fire. There can hardly be a doubt that these and several other fragments sent from Prienè to the British Museum belong to the colossal statue of Athenè Polias, described by Pausanias, and of which the remains of the pedestal were found in position inside the cella of the temple. *See* ante, p. 23. It is probable from the scale of the fragments that the figure of Athenè was about 20 feet high. The bronze wings belonged probably to a figure of Victory about 3 feet high, which may have stood on the hand of the Athenè.

Capital of an Ionic pilaster, from the temenos of Athenè Polias: on the face a floral ornament (anthemion) rests on a stem, from which issues on each side a tendril. On each return a similar pattern with shorter tendrils at the base a row of rosettes. This pattern extends over less than one-half of the return face on each side. The remainder of these return faces is sunk below the ground of the ornamented part. The whole is of very inferior workmanship to the rest of the architectural details and probably of a more modern age. On the sunk part of the right return is the following inscription:—

οἱ φυλέται Πανδι[ονίδος]
᾽Απολλωνίδην [τὸν δεῖνα]
ἀρετῆς ἕνεκα [τῆς εἰς]
αὐτο[ύς].

"The tribesmen of the tribe of Pandionis (dedicate this statue?) in honour of) Apollonides, on account of his services to the tribe."

This pilaster has a joint at the back. Height 1ft. 2½in., breadth 2ft. 3in.

C. T. N.

16. A BATTLE ON THE TEMPLE OF ATHENA, FROM A FRAGMENT IN THE BRITISH MUSEUM.
Height 1 foot 8 inches, Width 3 feet 1 inch.

DESCRIPTION OF PLATES.

PLATE I.
FRONTISPIECE.

Perspective view of the Temple of Minos Polias. Restored.

PLATES II. III. AND IV.
GENERAL PLANS.

These three Plates are engraved from drawings made on the spot by Mr. Edward Falkener, and faithfully represent the condition of the ruins as they existed when he visited the spot in 1845. Taken in conjunction with the two maps from the surveys of Mr W. Gell published by the Society in the first volume of the *Antiquities of Ionia*, they sufficiently explain the situation of Priene when it was a seaport, and below the Gulf of Latmos had been silted up by the detritus brought down by the River Maeander. It has been already pointed out, *ante*, p. 27, that the gradual destruction of its port from the advancement of the dry land in front of it was one, at least, of the principal causes of the decay of the city and of its ultimate abandonment.

PLATE V.
GENERAL PLAN OF THE TEMENOS OF THE TEMPLE.

Mr. Pullan found no traces of the six internal columns of the propylaeum indicated in Mr. Bedford's plan of that edifice engraved in the first volume of the *Antiquities of Ionia*, ch. ii. pl. 11. From the existence of columns in a similar situation in the two propylaea at Eleusis, which were probably of about the same date as this temple, it seems probable that internal pillars may have been introduced here also, though the building is smaller than either of the Eleusinian examples. The foundations, also, of pilasters which can be traced in the side-walls point also in the same direction. But whether this was the case or not, all trace of their previous existence has been removed from the floor of the edifice and their restoration cannot now be otherwise than conjectural.

Between the propylaeum and the temple Mr. Pullan found the foundations of a great rectangular block of masonry, measuring 45 feet by 23 (see his Report, *ante*, page 20), but he noticed nothing to indicate what the form of the superstructure might have been, nor the purpose, consequently, to which it was dedicated. It may have been a platform to provide an elevated site for an altar, though in that case—if its plan is correctly made out—it is difficult

to see where the steps were that must have led up to it. Or it may have been only a pedestal to support a group of sculpture. From the style of its architecture it is certainly more modern than the temple itself.

PLATE VI.
PLAN OF THE TEMPLE OF ATHENÉ POLIAS.

Though belonging to the smallest class of Greek hexastyle temples, its plan, measuring only 121 feet 8 inches by 64 feet, is one of the most complete and best proportioned of its class known to exist anywhere. The relative proportions of the cella to the pronaos and posticum and the arrangement of the peristyle are all typical, and unsurpassed for elegance by anything found elsewhere.

The position of the statue in the cella is clearly ascertained, and about 10 feet in front of it a metal screen or wall seems to have divided the cella into two nearly equal parts and to have protected the sacrarium from the promiscuous intrusion of worshippers.

The opisthodomus was enclosed, though in what manner was not clearly ascertained. The jambs of a doorway still exist between the two central pillars (pls. xiv. xvi. and xvii.), but it is not clear whether the two lateral openings were closed by an open metallic grill or by a screen of masonry, most probably the latter, as it would be a painful architectural bathos to close the centre from the public eye and leave the sides open. Nothing, however, was discovered to determine this question either way.

PLATES VII. AND VIII.
FRONT AND FLANK ELEVATIONS OF THE TEMPLE.

In all the restorations of this temple hitherto published the height of the columns has been assumed to be nine diameters, in accordance with the precept of Vitruvius (lib. iv. ch. 1); but it having been ascertained from the exhaustive analysis of Mr. Pearce (Appendix II.) that the real height was not less than ten diameters, the temple in these plates assumes a lighter and far more elegant form than has been hitherto suspected. This is even more apparent in the perspective view of the temple which forms the frontispiece to this volume. Ten diameters may now in fact be considered as about the normal proportion of Ionic columns of the best age. It is true, nevertheless, that those in the northern portion of the Erechtheum at Athens (without the plinth) do not exceed nine diameters in height, but they are spaced so widely apart and stand

* *Antiquities of Ionia, chap. ii. pls. 1 to 10; chap. iii. 1 to 9.*

1

so free that the stoutest possible proportion was there the most appropriate in an architectural sense, and the example does not consequently apply to any peristyle arrangement.

PLATES IX. AND X.

THE ORDER.

The order used at Priené is of a singularly pure and elegant class. It is perhaps not more elegant and is certainly less richly ornamented than that employed at the Smintheum, described further on (Plate xxix.), but for a monumental order applied to an edifice of such simplicity of outline as the Temple of Priené it seems inexceptionable.

The base with one bold torus fluted horizontally is perhaps preferable to one with two toruses, of nearly equal section as in the Smintheum, but as a rule taller and more ornamental bases seem generally to be a desideratum in the Ionic order. There is no novelty in the capital, but the plates clearly suggest the question whether or not it would be better that a metal fillet should be placed above the ogee moulding of the abacus. It seems certain that metal in some shape was introduced into the eye of the volute, and Messrs. Rayet and Thomas found traces of blue and red colour in various parts of the capital (Milet, &c. Plate 14), so that the gilding of a metal ornament seems almost indispensable to complete the harmony. This is the more probable on account of the unfinished unconstructive look of its present appearance. The metal fillet does not, however, so far as is known, occur elsewhere in such a position.

The entablature of the Smintheum has a considerable amount of additional ornament, and seems better to accord with the sculpture of its Zophorus than was the case at Priené. In the drawing (Plate ix.), where the sculpture of the frieze is omitted, the whole looks harmonious and appropriate, but with the sculpture introduced the plain lines of the architrave are hardly in keeping with the rest of the composition. In the Smintheum these defects have been avoided.

PLATE XI.

DETAILS OF THE ORDER.

A. Section of the base of the order drawn to the scale of 8 inches to 1 foot, or two-thirds the real size.

B. Apophysis of Inner order.

C. Cornice of a pedestal.

PLATE XII.

MOULDINGS.

Section of mouldings, partly belonging to the temple of Athené Polias, partly to objects found in the temenos whose original position could not be accurately ascertained.

PLATE XIII.

BASE AND CORNICE MOULDINGS OF PEDESTALS FROM PRONAOS.

A. Cornice of marble stelé, temenos.

B. Base of pedestal of statue.

C. Cornice of pedestal of statue.

D. Base of an oblong pedestal on north side of pronaos.

E. Cornice found in temenos.

F. Architrave of door in posticum.

G. Cornice found in temenos.

H. Base of stelé found in temenos.

I. Square base in temenos.

K. Base of pedestal found in pronaos.

PLATE XIV.

VIEW OF TEMPLE LOOKING EAST, FROM A PHOTOGRAPH.

Represents the appearance of the posticum after the site was cleared from the mass of fallen blocks which cumbered it. The outline of what was once the gulf of Latmus is seen in the distance. Most of it is now either marsh or partially cultivated land.

PLATE XV.

VIEW FROM PRONAOS LOOKING WEST.

Represents the appearance of the cella of the Temple when cleared out. The position of the pedestal of the colossal statue is clearly shown in the view, as well as that of the pedestals in the pronaos. The fronts of the two pillars of the posticum, which were prominent in the last plate, are seen over the cella walls. Beyond is the rocky ridge at the foot of which the Temple was situated. The whole is from a photograph.

PLATES XVI. AND XVII.

VIEWS OF THE POSTICUM.

Views of the remains of the posticum, from different points of view to a larger scale. Engraved from photographs.

PLATE XVIII.

CAPITALS OF ANTÆ.

The three upper figures in this Plate are engraved from photographs of fragments now in the British Museum. The fourth, or lowest figure, is a restoration of one of the capitals of the Antæ in so far as it can be, with certainty, made out.

It will be observed that in the centre of each of the acanthus leaves, from which the anthemion, or so-called honeysuckle ornament, springs, there is a sinking, more clearly seen in the marble than expressed in the engraving, of the three upper figures. From its form it seems almost certain that some metallic ornament was attached to the capital at this place, though of what shape and for what purpose it is now impossible to say. In its present state any such adjunct even if gilded would appear, no doubt, very tawdry and out of place, but when the whole was richly coloured, and many parts heightened by gilding, such an insertion might be employed not only in the most correct taste but so as to contribute to the artistic effect to an extent one can now hardly appreciate. That metal was used to heighten the effect of the capitals of the main order seems hardly doubtful, and if so its employment here seems only natural.

PLATE XIX.

FRAGMENTS OF A FRIEZE FOUND AT PRIENE.

This Plate gives four of the best preserved fragments of this frieze, of which, as has been already stated, ante, p. 30, many pieces were found in the ruins of the temple of Athené at Priené, and are now in the British Museum.

In the lower right hand corner of the Plate is a kneeling nude figure, winged, and with his lower extremities terminating in serpents. The right arm, now wanting, has been extended to the right, probably to avert a blow; a mantle is twisted round his left arm.

Though the head of this figure is wanting, the winged serpentode type shows that it represents a Giant, and a study of the numerous other fragments of this frieze leads to the conclusion that the subject was a Gigantomachia, in which doubtless Athené herself took a distinguished part. Height 1 ft. 2 in.

In the left hand lower corner of the Plate is a nude male figure, kneeling on his right knee. He appears to have been thrown down by an adversary standing over him on higher ground, who has drapery wound round his body and passing over his left shoulder. As the arms of both figures and the legs of the one on a higher level are wanting, it is very difficult to make out the action of the group, but, as part of a lion appears on the right of the victorious figure, it may be inferred that the group represents Dionysos striking down a Giant. Height of group 2 ft. 1½ in.

Above, in the right-hand corner, is a draped female figure moving rapidly to the right; the violence of her action is shown by the agitated folds of her drapery, which consists of a talaric chiton, over which is a mantle cast over both arms, the ends flying behind her. Her head, left hand, and forearm nearly to the elbow, and right arm from the elbow, are wanting. The feet, which wear sandals, stand on a projecting ledge. Height 1 ft. 11 in.

In the left-hand upper corner is the torso of a draped female figure also moving rapidly to the right, and clad in a talaric chiton and mantle similarly composed. Her head, feet, right arm, and left arm from above the elbow are wanting. Height 1 ft. 8 in.

Many more fragments of this frieze were collected at Priene, and are now in the British Museum. In examining these fragments the following peculiarities may be noted. They are for the most part hammer-dressed at the back with a thickness ranging from 2½ to 6 inches. The figures generally stand on rocky ground or on a projecting ledge, below which the marble is wrought as a plain margin varying in width from 9 to 5 inches. The joints are roughly finished, and, so far as can be inferred from the evidence of these details, the frieze does not seem suitable to have formed part of the principal external order of the temple.

PLATE XX.

TWO IONIC HEADS.

Colossal female head, broken off from a statue at the base of the neck. The lower part of the nose, both eyes, and the left temple, have been much injured, and the left upper lip has suffered slightly. Above the forehead is a triple row of formal curls. The remainder of the hair is concealed under a close-fitting cap, on which, when first discovered, were traces of ornaments painted in brown. The curls on the right side of the head have been painted red; on the other side their surface has been blackened by the action of fire. The resemblance of this head to the one found on the site of the Mausoleum (Newton, History of Discoveries, ii. part 1. p. 103, plate 2) is so marked as to make it certain that they are both the work of the same school, if not of the same artist. The execution of the

Priene head is very masterly, all but the curls, which are very roughly indicated, while those of the Mausoleum head are carefully wrought in spirals. Height 1 ft. 3½ in.

Ionic male head, which has been fitted on to a statue at the base of the neck. Only the left side of the face, including part of the right nostril and nearly all the right side of the mouth, are preserved. The right side and the back of the head behind the ear have been split off. The portrait represents a middle-aged man, closely shaven, and bald over the forehead; his hair is short and slightly waved; the lips are thin and compressed with an expression of strong will, the chin broad with a depression in the middle, the nose broad, widening towards the tip, which is broken away; the eye is deep set, the circle of the iris has been marked by red colour, of which there are still traces. The brow has been contracted. The features are finely modelled, and the work belongs to a good period. The portrait may represent one of the Diadochi, and bears some resemblance to one of the kings of Bithynia as represented on coins, but there is no trace of a diadem. The surface of the marble is discoloured, as if by fire. When found, this head was in three fragments. Height 1 ft. 3½ in.

PLATE XXI.

PEDESTAL.

Front and side views of a square pedestal found in the temenos. On the front and back is sculptured in relief a floral ornament (anthemion) rising from a stem, out of which spring acanthus leaves. On either side stands a gryphon, his right paw raised and resting on the volute above the acanthus leaves. On either return face of the pedestal is a floral ornament issuing from a stem, out of which spring on either side acanthus leaves and spiral tendrils, terminating in half anthemia. This pattern is surmounted by a bold projecting moulding, corresponding to the abacus of a pilaster, below which is an ornament corresponding to the pulvinar and volute of an Ionic pilaster.[1] On the top of the pedestal are two deep sinkings, one of which is oblong, the other is shape something like a rocket. These probably served as the support of some votive offering in metal. The sides of these sinkings are roughly hewn away, probably to enable some spoller to detach the object which stood on the pedestal.[2]

[1] N. Roget, Abbé et le Golfe Antiolyse, p. 34, describes another similar pedestal which he found in the ruins at Priene, between the Propylaea and the Pronaos; see his Plate 17, figs. 1, 2. The height of the example is the Museum is 2ft. 6in. by 1ft. 6in. each way.

[2] It appears to me probable that it was originally designed as an altar, the upper part being in bronze, or some other metal-work. F.

ARCHITECTURE BY J. F.
SCULPTURE BY C. T. N.

CHAPTER II.

TEOS.

Teos, now Sighajik, was an Ionian city on the south shore of the isthmus which connects the peninsula of Karaburun with the mainland, and which is bounded on the north by the Gulf of Smyrna. The site of Teos was one which could not fail to commend itself to the Greek adventurers, who, at a very early period, established themselves on the west coast of Asia Minor, wherever a safe anchorage could be combined with a strongly fortified position. At Teos, as at Mytilene, Knidos, Phokaa, Myndos, a promontory, connected with the mainland by an isthmus, formed the natural protection of two harbours, opening respectively north and south, and by cutting a canal through this isthmus a double harbour was formed which admitted of a choice of entry and egress according to the prevailing wind.[1] The northernmost of these harbours, the ancient Portus Gerasticus, is described by Hamilton[2] as accessible at all times and with almost all winds; the port on the south is now almost filled up with sand.

The first Greek settlers at Teos are said to have been Orchomenian Minyæ under Athamas.[3] Here, as elsewhere on the same coast, the Greeks found the Karians already established, who do not, however, appear to have been so hostile to the new comers at Teos as was the case at Ephesos and other places; indeed, there is evidence from a Teian inscription, as Boekh and Grote have shown, that the indigenous population must have been gradually fused and amalgamated with Hellenic immigrants.[4] The original settlement founded by the Minyæ was reinforced about the time of the Ionian migration by Athenians led by Nauklos and Damasos, sons of Kodrus. Beotia contributed other colonists under Geres.[5] The tradition of these Athenian immigrants was preserved at Teos for many centuries in the names of their demes, or πύργος.[6] The Portus Gerasticus owed its name to the Baotian leader, Geres.

Teos, like Priene, was one of the twelve Ionian cities which, in very early times, formed a league or confederacy with a common place of meeting, the Panionion near Priene, where there was a temple of Poseidon Helikonios.[7] In a position so favourable for navigation as Teos, the spirit of maritime enterprise must have been early developed, and accordingly we find that this was one of the favoured Græco-Asiatic cities which, in the sixth century B.C., were admitted by the Egyptian king, Amasis, to the privilege of trading at Naukratis, and that the Teians took a leading part in founding the Helledon there.[8]

Their prosperity seems to have continued unimpaired till the 59th Olympiad (B.C. 544-541), when, in common with the other cities of Ionia, Teos was subdued by Harpagos, the General of Cyrus. After their city had thus lost its independence, a portion of the Teians migrated to Thrace, where they founded Abdera (B.C. 544), but the majority of the citizens must have remained after the capture of their city, for we find that not many years afterwards the Teians contributed a contingent of seventeen ships to the naval forces during the Ionian revolt against Darius.[9] Moreover we learn from an epigram of Simonides that the Teian poet Anacreon, who flourished B.C. 559-25, was buried in his native city,[10] which could hardly have been the case had it been totally abandoned then.

---

[1] For the topography of Teos and its harbours see Lévy, xxviii. 27, 28; G. Weisbfeld in the Berlin *Archäol. Zeitung*, 1876, pp. 24-302. As the two ports were connected by a canal through the isthmus, Pliny's statement, *Hist. Nat.* v. 31, § 138, that Teos was built on an island, becomes intelligible. For a general panorama of the coast near Teos see Léon de Laborde, *Voyage de l'Asie Mineure*, pl. xliii.

[2] *Travels in Asia Minor*, ii. pp. 14-15; Lévy, loc. cit.

[3] Müller, *Orchomenos*, p. 303; Herod. i. 146. In a fragment of inscription, Boekh, *Corpus Inscr.* No. 3079, the name Athamas occurs. Boekh conjectures that this is a fragment of an honorary degree or dedication in which occur ... οἰκιστὴς τῶ Ἀθάμαν, a new founder of the city.

[4] Pausan. vii. 3, § 3; Boekh, *Corpus Inscr.* No. 3064; Grote, *Hist.* iii. 251.   [5] Boekh, *Corpus Inscr.* No. 3064.

[6] Strabo, xiv. p. 633; Pausan. loc. cit.

[7] Herod. i. 142, 148.

[8] Ibid. ii. 178; Grote, iii. pp. 449-52, who gives reasons for thinking that the Greek factory at Naukratis was founded before the reign of Amasis.

[9] Herod. vi. 8.; K. F. Hermann, *Alterthümer*, p. 96.

[10] Bergk, *Poet. Lyrici*, 1843, p. 581, No. 118.

After the suppression of the Ionian revolt Teos was sacked by the Persians,[11] but after the defeat of Xerxes it probably recovered some of its ancient prosperity. After the establishment of the Athenian maritime empire Teos became one of its dependencies, and we find its name among the Ionian cities in the tribute lists.[12] With a view, probably, of establishing a strong outpost at Teos, the Athenians built a wall there to defend the city from attacks from the interior. This wall was probably built across the isthmus. The decline of Athenian power after the failure of the Sicilian expedition led to the revolt of Chios and other Ionian cities, B.C. 412. This induced the Teians to waver in their allegiance, and after some hesitation they admitted within their walls the troops of the neighbouring cities, Klazomenae and Erythrae, which had joined in the revolt against Athens. These Klazomenians and Erythraeans were supported by a Persian force sent to Teos by Tissaphernes, and through their combined efforts the wall built by the Athenians was demolished and the city rendered defenceless on the land side.[13]

The Athenians, however, must have reasserted their rule very soon after this, for, according to Diodorus, Teos was taken from them by the Lacedaemonians, B.C. 406.[14]

After the death of Alexander the Great, Teos passed into the hands of Antigonus (B.C. 306—301), by whose despotic edict the population was augmented through the forcible transplantation into it of the inhabitants of the neighbouring city Lebedos. The mode of procedure by which this arbitrary change was to be wrought is set forth in the long and interesting inscription in which this edict has been handed down to us, and which contains many curious details showing how much the autonomy of the Greek cities was encroached upon by the military rulers who succeeded to the Empire of Alexander. The edict ordains that a new code of laws suitable to the altered conditions of the amalgamated communities is to be framed; in the meantime the Lebedians are allowed to adopt the laws of Kos, careful provision is made for the housing of the new comers from Lebedos, and their ancient rights and privileges are expressly guaranteed.[15]

Teos was one of the Ionian cities which submitted to Prepelaos, the general of Lysimachus, B.C. 302.[16] There seems to be evidence from an inscription that it subsequently passed under the dominion of the Seleukidae.[17] After the defeat of Antiochus the Great by the Romans, B.C. 190, Teos became part of the dominions of the Kings of Pergamos. After the death of Attalus III. B.C. 138—133, Teos with the rest of his kingdom was transferred to Rome.

It was during the time when Teos formed part of the Attalid kingdom that it became celebrated as the principal seat of Dionysiac worship in Ionia.[18] In the period of the Diadochi, when the interest in politics decayed with the loss of liberty, the love of scenic and musical entertainments became an absorbing passion among the Asiatic Greeks, and especially in Ionia.

In that part of Asia Minor was formed a great company or guild of actors, who styled themselves "the Dionysiac artists," and had, as the directors of great musical and dramatic festivals, enjoyed the special protection and patronage of the Pergamene kings and probably of the Diadochi, their predecessors. Teos, the birthplace of Anacreon and the home of lyric music, was pre-eminently the seat of this worship, the celebrity and importance of which is attested by a number of extant decrees, one of the earliest of which can be fixed to B.C. 193.[19]

We learn from these inscriptions that the Teians claimed to have enjoyed, from an ancient date, peculiar privileges and immunities, such as the inviolability of territory and the right of sanctuary, and they appealed at this epoch to the Greek cities generally to have these privileges renewed or confirmed. The decrees of twenty-six states in answer to this petition have been preserved; in these decrees all that the Teians claim is solemnly guaranteed to them. The powerful protection of the Ætolian league formed one of these guarantees.

Three Teian inscriptions commemorate the good deeds of one Kraton, a flute-player, who was elected by the Dionysiac artists priest and president of their festival. The inscriptions recount his liberality in fulfilling these functions, and his great influence with the kings of Pergamos, with Delphi, and with other Greek states. In consideration of these services the decree orders that one statue of Kraton be set up at Teos, another at Delos, and a third wherever Kraton may direct. The date of these decrees falls within the reigns of Eumenes II. and Attalus II., Philadelphos, B.C. 197-137.[20]

Strabo states that the Dionysiac artists abandoned Teos in consequence of a revolution, στάσις, and fled to Ephesus; that Attalus afterwards established them in Myonnesus, between Teos and Lebedos; and that in

[11] Suidas, s. v. Ἀναχρέων. [12] Kohler, Urkunden zur Geschichte d. Delisch-Attischen Bundes, p. 101.

[13] Thucyd. viii. 16, 20. [14] Diodorus, xiii. 76.

[15] Waddington-Lebas, Inscriptions Grecques, &c. iii. partie 5, No. 86. [16] Droysen, Hellenismus, ii. 292.

[17] G. Hirschfeld, Archäol. Zeitung, &c. 60, p. 26.

[18] Hirschfeld, ibid. p. 26; Lüders, Die Dionys. Künstler, pp. 24, 80; Bockh, Corpus Inscr. No. 3067; Hermes, ix. 501; Fessart, De Teïenis Actif. Paris, 1873, pp. 7, 18, 22, 26, 32.

[19] Hirschfeld, loc. cit. p. 26; Waddington-Lebas, Inscriptions Grecques, gr. iii. partie 5, p. 29.

[20] Bockh, Corpus Inscr. ii. p. 637c, and Nos. 3067-70; Lüders, pp. 75-80.

consequence of the objections of the Teians they were transferred by the Romans to Lebedos, where they still were in the time of Strabo.[74] It is to be presumed that the Attalos referred to by the geographers was the third king of that name, who died B.C. 133. The Dionysiac artists, therefore, could not have been transferred to Myonnesus later than that year. As we have no further information about the revolution which led to their flight from Teos, the date of that event cannot be only approximately fixed as having taken place before the death of Attalus III. It seems probable, as Dr. Hirschfeld suggests,[75] that the sumptuous temple of Dionysos, of which Hermogenes was the architect, was planned, if not completed, between B.C. 193, when there was evidently a revival of the Dionysiac worship at Teos, and B.C. 133, when the revolution which transferred the artists to Myonnesus had certainly taken place. On the other hand, there is clear evidence that in the Imperial period a revival of the Dionysiac worship took place at Teos,[76] and the temple explored by Mr. Pullan may have been either restored or wholly rebuilt in Roman times, as he supposes. This is confirmed by the word ΑΥΤΟΚΡΑΤΩΡ, which Mr. Pullan copied on a piece of architrave in the ruins (see post, p. 39). This may be part of the same dedicatory inscription of which Dr. Hirschfeld found two fragments in the ruins of the temple, and which, from the form of the letters, he considers to be certainly not earlier than the middle of the third century B.C., but which may be much later.[77]

C. T. NEWTON.

---

[74] Strabo, xiv. 643; Luders, pp. 85, 86. Foucart (De Collegiis Scen. Art. p. 22) suggests that the cause of the revolution at Teos was an attempt on the part of the Dionysiac artists to usurp the functions of the citizens. According to Plutarch, Anton. 57, M. Antonius established Dionysiac artists at Priene. A fragment of inscription, Boeckh, Corpus, No. 3068, may be part of a decree made by some proconsul or king in reference to these transfers of the Dionysiac artists, as Boeckh conjectures.

[75] Hirschfeld, loc. cit. p. 29. The date of Hermogenes is unknown; see Brunn, Geschichte d. Griech. Künstler, ii. p. 358.

[76] See Boeckh, Corpus, No. 3062, and Foucart, De Colleg. p. 9. An unedited inscription, brought from Teos by Mr. Pullan and presented by the Society to the British Museum, contains more than one decree relating to a Dionysiac thiasos. This is probably of the third century. On a Teian copper coin of Agrippina (Mionnet, Supp. vi. p. 364, No. 1015) Dionysos is represented within a tetrastyle temple; and the type of this God occurs constantly on Imperial coins down to the time of Valerian.

[77] Hirschfeld, loc. cit. On one of these fragments he read τ]οῦ Διον[ύσου, on the other Μητρ[οδ]ώρου.

MR. PULLAN'S REPORT ON EXCAVATIONS AT TEOS.

Upon hearing that the Society of Dilettanti had granted funds for the exploration of the Temple of Bacchus at Teos, I commenced making preparations for departure from Smyrna. Spiro, the dragoman recommended by Mr. Consul Blunt—who had accompanied me when I made the preliminary survey of the coast agreed to attend me on this occasion also. The Smyrna and Aidin Railway Company supplied me with tools, and the timber required for the erection of a storehouse was purchased in the town.

The timber and tackle filled a small caique, which I dispatched in Spiro's charge with instructions to sail round the Cape of Karaburun at the mouth of the Gulf of Smyrna to the Bay of Sighajik, the town near which lay the ruins of Teos. The caique sailed on March 13, 1862.

I left Smyrna on April 3, proceeding by land round the shores of the gulf; I reached Sighajik on the following day. Owing to contrary winds, the caique with tents had not arrived, so I applied to my old acquaintance the yuzbashi for a house. Here we remained until the 7th, when the tents arrived, and the tents were pitched before nightfall.

The ruins of the city of Teos stand on a peninsula which slopes gently towards the S.E. The heap of marbles which marked the site of the Temple of Bacchus lay in the centre of the city, the boundary walls of which could be distinctly traced throughout their entire circuit. The site of the temple was covered with bushes and stood in the centre of a cornfield.

Having made the necessary arrangements with the proprietor of the field we commenced operations by cutting down the brushwood. This was accomplished by the 9th. Three excavations were commenced at the N.W. corner, where a portion of the pavement was visible, one plinth being then in situ. On carrying a trench parallel to the steps, the pavement of the peristyle was found in position to a distance of 45 feet. The plinths which stood on this pavement had been removed. (See the plan, Plate xxii.)

By April 14 we had reached the N.E. angle, where we found that the peristyle and steps had been all carried away. This being the most accessible quarter these stones had, doubtless, been removed for building purposes. Subsequently we found that this was the case on the whole of the E. front.

On the 30th the men were set to work on the S. side to cut a trench beyond the line of the steps for the purpose of removing any portion of the frieze that might have fallen there. Several slabs were found representing a Dionysiac procession, but executed in a late and rude style of art. On the N. side some courses of the cella wall were found in situ, and also a considerable portion of the pavement of the peristyle. On the S. side on the contrary the steps had been removed, and the lower courses only remained. The mouldings of the bases found on this side were inferior in execution to those on the N., pointing to a rebuilding of this portion of the edifice at a later period.

On the 22nd we dug pits at the N. and W. sides in order

to discover whether the pavement of the peristyle was in existence. At a depth of three feet the workmen came to a layer of broken tiles and pottery, and at a depth of 5ft. 6in. to courses of flint which may have formed a foundation for a better sort of pavement. During the excavation we found a corner stone of the pediment.

About this time the governor of the principal town in the district, Sevri Hissar, sent a hekji or watchman to see that I did not remove any treasure. The hekji informed me that fourteen years before a party of English sailors dug on the site of the Temple till they came to a gate, beyond which they could see vessels of gold, but that when they had reached this interesting point they were driven away by magical spirits.

By May 10 the pavement and the foundations of the cella were laid bare, and by the 23rd the earth from the interior of the cella was all removed, and it was found that about two-thirds of the pavement of the cella remained. The foundation course, which formed the bed of the upper pavement, was visible throughout the remaining area. The whole surface of the pavement was strewn with fragments of earthenware tiles without any admixture of marble mouldings. From this it is to be inferred that the roof had been of wood covered with tiles. The walls of the posticum had been lined with slabs of white marble.

On June 11 an English brig came into the harbour of Sighajik to land with colours. This was a most unusual occurrence, and it afforded an opportunity for sending to England a slab of the frieze found on the site of the temple of Bacchus.[*]

On the 12th, after considerable opposition from the Turkish authorities, I got the slab on board. On the 16th the medjlis or town council of Sevri Hissar rode to our encampment and threatened to disembark the slab by main force. They also wrote to the Pasha of Smyrna to complain. His reply however was to the effect that I had not violated the terms of the firman, and for the future I was left unmolested.

After this I set thirty men to work at the E. end of the temple. Here it was found that all the steps had been taken away, but the pavement of the area in front of the temple was discovered; it had been bounded by a low wall, or more probably by seats, one of which was found in situ.

A portion of the architrave of the portico was here brought to light, with an inscription upon it, one word of which, ΑΠΠΟΚΡΑΤΗΣ, was distinctly visible. This confirmed my opinion that the temple had been rebuilt in Roman times.

From the 26th of June to the 7th of July the men were employed on the peristyle. At a distance of 33 ft. on the S. side traces of a Roman Doric colonnade were found, referring to the W. at about 66 ft. from the steps of the temple. The distance from centre to centre of the

[*] See Pl. xxx. This slab was presented by the Society of Dilettanti to the British Museum.

columns was 7 ft. 10 in. At the S.W. angle the voussoirs of an arch were found, probably belonging to a gate in the outer wall.

The same flinty foundation was found on all sides; upon it there was probably a pavement ranging with the projection found beneath the steps on N. and S.W. sides. This projection is shown on the plan and elevations, Plates xxii.—xxiv.

On the 9th of July, the excavations being completed, we returned to Smyrna by land.

Remarks on the Mode of Construction and data for the Restoration.

It is evident from the plan that this Temple was not that erected by Hermogenes and described by Vitruvius as being Exastyle.[*]

[*] * * Hujus exemplar (scilicet) Ionici Romæ nullum habemus, sed in Asiâ Teo hexastylon labro Patri. Eas enim rationes exemplaribus constituit Hermogenes, qui etiam primus Hexastylon Pseudo-dipteris ratiocinationem in

The inferior character of the sculptures on the frieze, and the inscription on the architrave, prove that it was rebuilt in Roman times. There is a certain degree of inequality in the workmanship; for instance, the contours of the mouldings of the bases on the N. side are superior to those on the S., which seems to confirm the idea of a reconstruction.

Some of the plinths—the steps on the N. and W. sides and the pavement and foundation of cella, having been found in position, the dimensions of the temple were ascertained without difficulty.

All the members of the order were recovered as well as various pediment stones,[†] but the drums of columns were so few in number that the exact height of the column must be a matter of conjecture.

The Temple was built of grey marble, obtained at a quarry about three miles to the N.W. In this quarry there are still several blocks with Ionian numerals inscribed upon them.[‡]

[†] For the details of the order see Plate xxv.

[‡] See Hamilton, Asia Minor, ii. pp. 17–19.

DESCRIPTION OF PLATES.

Plate XXII.

PLAN OF THE TEMPLE AT TEOS.

The temple at Teos is the smallest of the three described in this volume, measuring only 112 feet by 58 feet from the angle of the plinths of the outer column, and consequently covering only 6,496 square feet as compared with the 7,816 of the temple at Priene, and the 9,513 of the Smintheum. The arrangements are very similar to those at Priene, but the more contracted dimensions of the Teos temple and the general meanness and poverty-stricken look which characterize it contrast very unfavourably with the plan of either of the other two temples.

The parts shaded darkly on the plan are those of which the foundation remained sufficiently distinct for Mr. Pullan to ascertain their position with certainty. The parts shaded more lightly are interpolated, but enough remained to enable this to be done without the risk of any appreciable error of sufficient importance to be remarked.

Plates XXIII. AND XXIV.

FRONT AND FLANK ELEVATION.

The front and flank elevations of the temples at Teos show the same poverty of appearance that characterizes the plan. The order has no especial beauty in itself, and the pillars are too widely spaced for dignity or strength.

Owing to the slope of the ground a noble flight of twelve steps leads up to the front portico, but the six steps on the

flank seem neither to possess the dignified repose of the three steps at Priene, nor of the ten which, if properly broken up by perpendicular parts, must have added so much to the imposing grandeur of the Smintheum.

Plate XXV.

THE ORDER AT TEOS.

The appearance of the order goes far to justify the suspicion that the temple must have been rebuilt in Roman times, though the architect must have still followed, no doubt, the traditions of a better age. The base, however, is very much more like several that occur in later times than the elegant even if somewhat unconstructive form which prevailed in the great Grecian age, and the capital is characterized by the hard horizontal line between the volutes of the Roman capital, instead of the elegant downward curve which is universally found in the Greek capitals. The upper moulding of the architrave is more richly ornamented than is usually the case, but in this instance seems disproportioned to either the poverty of the capital below or to that of the cornice above it; while the echinus, though its form is copied from a good age, betrays an unskilful hand in its execution.

The smaller order seems to belong to a slightly better and earlier age, but the fragments of it are too slight to admit of any satisfactory appreciation of its characteristics.

J. F.

CHAPTER III.

THE SMINTHIUM.

In the autumn of 1853, Captain, now Admiral, Spratt, when conducting the Admiralty Survey on the coast of the Troad, discovered the site of the Temple of Apollo Smintheus, which Strabo describes as situated in the Hamaxitia, a district forming a triangle at the south-western end of the Troad, of which the base is the course of the river Tuzla (probably the ancient Satnioeis), and the apex Cape Baba, the ancient Lectum. The Hamaxitia was the district of Hamaxitos, one of the old towns of this part of the Troad which contributed to people the new city founded by Antigonus about the year 310 B.C., and augmented by Lysimachus, who changed its name from Antigoneia to Alexandreia.

The remains of the temple are situated at a short distance from the sea-shore, twelve geographical miles in direct distance to the south of the ruins of Alexandreia, and four geographical miles to the north-east of Cape Lectum. "They are adjacent," writes Admiral Spratt, "to a Turkish village named Kulagli, standing on a low ridge, which falls gradually to the plain and river of Tuzla.[1] Several fragments of marble scattered about the village induced me to inquire for the place from which they were brought: there was much reluctance to satisfy me, some directing me to the plain of Tuzla and elsewhere, but the offer of a few piastres at length induced a Turk to point to a small *plateau*, which connects the village ridge with another running parallel to it, and not more than ten minutes' walk below where I stood. Here I came suddenly upon the remains of a large temple, consisting chiefly of columns lying in all directions within two or three small gardens, or on the road side, or in the stone enclosures. Some of the columns in the gardens appeared to be standing *in situ*, but no more than a few feet of them appeared above ground; there were also some massive foundations of the temple near them. Not less than forty fragments or portions of the columns lay upon the site or in the vicinity. They were fluted, of white marble, and apparently Ionic, though not a single portion of any capital was to be found. The diameter of the shaft was four feet immediately above the base. Two springs of excellent water rise on the *plateau* near the site of the temple, one of which issues from a small cavern. Adjoining the temple are some ruins of a large building of Roman times, with walls formed in part of horizontal courses of brick. Further on is an isolated buttress, belonging to another large building. These two ruins are nearly twenty feet high. There are some indications also of a church and small town scattered over the plateau, but without any appearance of town walls. The situation is in a hollow between two ridges. Upon the western ridge there is a road to the sea-coast, which it meets three or four miles to the northward of Cape Baba. Upon this road are five or six sarcophagi, lying on their sides or half-buried in the soil: they are formed of a dark volcanic rock, a species of trachyte, similar to that of Assos, among the ruins of which ancient city we find it used for the same purpose. On the shore where the road terminates are several fragments of the temple, which have no doubt been brought thus far for the purpose of embarkation, and to be used in some modern building. On the top of the ridge of Kulagli, on the edge of the plain of Tuzla, I found a circular pedestal of white marble, sculptured with festoons of flowers between bulls' heads, the whole originally well executed; it was probably brought here from Kulagli, as there is no other ancient fragment within a mile of it."[2]

It may be noticed that the temple stood about halfway on the road that St. Paul travelled when he left his ship at Alexandria Troas and went afoot to Assos, where he rejoined it and his companions.

---

[1] This plain is the Halesium of Strabo (xiii. p. 604), a word of the same meaning as the Turkish Tuzla, and so named from some copious but saline source, described by Strabo as ἐν Ὑρμεραίῳ χωρίῳ ἀλυκαῖσιν, εἰς Ἑρμαῖον τρεφόμενον πρὸς Ἀπόλλῳⁱ. Tragasae stood probably at the modern Tuzla; a little below this village the shallow ponds into which the water of the sources is collected, and evaporated by the summer heat and breezes northerly winds—See Hunt in Walpole's *Memoirs*, i. p. 153.

[2] *Transactions of the Royal Society of Literature*, vol. v. new series, pp. 236-243.

The worship of Apollo under the title Smintheus, by which Chryses appeals to him ("Iliad," i. 39), was very general about this region.[1] The name was associated with a barbarian or provincial name for mouse (σμίνθος, Hesychius), and connected, as usual, with various mythical stories; and Apollo Smintheus as queller of a plague of mice, or the sender of mice who gnawed bow-strings and shield-straps, is shown on coins with a mouse in his hand; and a statue of the god by Scopas in this very temple—mentioned by Strabo and Eustathius—had a mouse below its foot.[2]

The magnitude and importance of the temple prove the celebrity of the oracle here, of which the sibyl Herophilé is said to have been the priestess;[3] and an inscription, of which Mr. Pullan sent home a rubbing, records a dedication to Apollo under the local title, together with Artemis and Latona.

This inscription runs thus:— "Under the sacred presidentship of Babius son of Pagmenes from the revenue of the moneys consecrated by Lochus son of Kallimedes, to Apollo Xmitheus Artemis, and Latona." The orthography Xmitheus, instead of Smintheus, is a local peculiarity which occurs also on the coins of Alexandria Troas.[4]

The Sminthium was of better material and larger scale, as well as finer in architectural style, than the temple excavated by the Society at Teos and described in the preceding chapter. Both are Ionic, but the Sminthium has eight columns in front, instead of six, and they are of much larger dimensions; like the Teos temple, however, it appears to have been commenced and carried to a certain point with more elaborate skill and fuller resources than were available to the end, and the workmanship of the mouldings was not in every part of uniform excellence. What remained of the damaged sculpture of the frieze showed little trace of excellence of any kind. The date of the best parts of the structure probably falls within the century preceding Alexander the Great.

The first feeling on turning over the show of results in the transmitted drawings might well be akin to something like dismay. It is not merely that the structure was, as anticipated, a dilapidated ruin,—the heap that was expected to contain the architectural members proved to consist chiefly of a massive and denuded basement, and the very ruins seemed to have vanished.

It happened that the commencement of the excavation was more fruitful than any other portion, owing to the existence of a road at the part first disturbed, which had covered up permanently, and so preserved, many important stones. But for this encouragement at the beginning, it is probable that Mr. Pullan would have soon desisted, and transferred his operations, as was arranged should be done in such case, to another site. All drawbacks and disadvantages notwithstanding, it is fortunate that he was led on to search the entire site thoroughly.

When surface soil and gardens were cleared away, the massive platform foundation of the temple was laid bare to the extent of some 100 feet by 160 in length, and found to consist of a compact base and core of large blocks of limestone and ragstone cramped together and run with lead; but all was so utterly denuded of marble casing and proper superstructure that only a single stone of one lower course of a wall was in position, and only a few feet of three actual marble steps at one spot were undisturbed, out of a range of ten steps that originally ran all round the building. (See Plan, Plate xxvi.)

Nevertheless, there appears, after careful comparison of the drawings, good ground for confidence that from the lines given by these stones and in the foundation, as well as from the beds of the stones above them and their heights, both ground plan and profile of steps and stylobate have been satisfactorily recovered.

Again, the details of the foundations exhibit the directions and divisions of the cella walls, and demonstrate for the most part certainly the number and places of the columns upon the pavement above it, although the actual slabs on which they were placed have disappeared. The accuracy of the spacing of the columns as shown in Plate xxvi. thus deduced was open to verification by comparison with the one or two architrave stones which were fortunately found complete; as more than one or two were found, but even that number if they are perfect are as conclusive as they are welcome.

In like manner, only one or two capitals and bases of columns remained to represent the forty repetitions of these parts that composed the original peristyle.

By a singular piece of good fortune, all the drums belonging to one column except the uppermost were found; and as the lower diameter of the missing drum is given by the upper diameter of the drum on which it rested, and its upper diameter is given by the circle of the capital it sustained or the soffit of the architrave

[1] Pausanias, x. 12, s. 3, p. 827   [2] Strabo, xiii. p. 604; Politia, Sketos, pp. 109-13.
[3] Herophilé prophesied about Samos, Claros, Delos, and at Delphi, where Pausanias was shown the rock which she stood upon.
[4] The worship of Apollo Smintheus was located at Tenedos, Hamaxitus in Æolis, in Rhodes, Crete, Sicily, and Teos, near Corinth. Urlichs, Skopas, p. 109. De Witte in Revue Numismatique, N.S. iii. Paris, 1858.

these elements, with the continued line of diminution, must give the height of the column within very narrow limits of error.

The dimensions and profiles of the members of the entablature and pediment are fully recovered, and thus the order and elevation may be considered as complete, as shown in Plates xxvii. and xxviii.

Some proportions of the smaller columns within the peristyle seem recoverable; and there is no uncertainty, at least on plan, regarding the proportions of the pronaos, naos, and opisthodomos.

The temple, in technical language, is Ionic Octostyle, with fourteen columns only on the sk; fifteen or even sixteen would be more in accordance with ordinary practice and the formula of Vitruvius, but every new discovery of good Greek work proves how independent the art was of inflexible rules. The spacing of the columns is pycnostyle, or one and a half diameters apart, which, according to Vitruvius, is the closest order that was admissible in good architecture, and so probably it was in Roman orders, but in Grecian Doric one diameter is not unusual, and even in the Parthenon 1·38 is the spacing employed. Strictly speaking the pillars at the Sminthium are 1·523, or a little more than one and a half diameter apart, but are even then in curious contrast with those of the temple at Teos. These latter are of the diastyle order, or the widest that Vitruvius admits of, being a little more than three diameters apart (3·166). It is an arrangement, however, of which he disapproves in consequence of the liability of the epistylia to crack and break when the supports are so distant.¹ In practice the objection did not apply, in this instance at least, the pillars of the Sminthium being only 9·70½ feet apart from centre to centre, those of the temple at Teos, 10·7; the excess being less than one foot and the epistylium being still considerably under the length employed in other temples. It is just one of those many instances, alluded to in the Introduction, in which the Greek architects showed such a perfect appreciation of what was most appropriate under the circumstances. When first introduced—and there is every reason to suppose that the Sminthium was an early example—every one must have felt the extreme incongruence of the pseudo-dipteral arrangement, as compared with the double range of columns of the true dipteral form. They consequently crowded their pillars as closely together as the rules of the art admitted of to remedy the defect. At Teos, on the contrary, though the temple was smaller, the single range of columns was so close to the walls of the cella that they gave it all the support required, and the widest possible spacing could introduce no apparent weakness.

The main point of interest in the Sminthium is that it furnishes a rare and also a peculiar example of the pseudo-dipteral arrangement. This, as defined by architectural writers, consists in omitting the inner row of columns both in the fronts and flanks of the temple, retaining only those of the pronaos and posticum, by which means great additional spaciousness is gained to the ambulatory. It is scarcely to be supposed, as Vitruvius suggests, that this was a mere economical scheme for making one row of columns do duty for two. Such a trick would have been the idlest of failures; the omission, manifest from every point of view that a Greek would have considered, must have been a difference counted on and calculated to give emphasis to the fronts. It may, however, have been, as suggested above (p. 7), that it was designed to allow the paintings, with which there is every reason to believe the cella walls were adorned, to be seen with greater facility, or to allow larger and more consecutive pictures being used for that purpose than were introduced in earlier times. From certain details in the foundations it might be presumed, though not with certainty, that in this temple an inner range of columns existed on the fronts; this however is not sufficiently clear to justify their insertion on the plan.

Vitruvius describes this form of temple, and refers to two examples of it,—one at Magnesia, by the inventor, Hermogenes of Alabanda, the architect to whom he ascribes the erection of a temple at Teos. This, as mentioned ante (p. 15), was measured by M. Texier in 1842, and the drawings are now in course of publication by MM. Ravet and Thomas in their work on Milet et le Golfe Latmique. Vitruvius then refers to another temple, but in terms that are not so much enigmatical as corrupt, and more likely to conceal a reference to the edifice we are discussing than to any other. The text has been variously tampered with, but the original reading, "Ædes Apollinis nuncto," is meaningless, and seems to at least as much like Sminthei as a Menerthe facta into which it has been transformed by editors. (See Schneider's note.)²

A detailed examination of the design, so far as the materials admit of this being done, has made it evident that the architect of the Sminthium was master to some extent of the same theory of proportional design which has been developed in detail at Athens, Bassae, and elsewhere, though the state of ruin in which Mr. Pullan

---

¹ Vitruvius, III. 2 and 3.

² "Pseudodipteros autem sic collocatur ut in fronte et postico octo columnæ sonsint, in lateribus cum angulartibus quindecim, sint autem parietes cellæ contra quatuordm columnas medianas in frontis et postico. Ita spatium intercolumniorum et lati circuitionis columnas spatium erit a parietibus cum extremis ordinibus columnarum. Hujus exemplar Romæ non est, sed Magnesiæ Dianæ Hermogenis Alabandi et Apollinis a Menerthe facta."—Vitruvius, iii. 2.

found the remains was such that it would hardly be safe to rely much on any induction that might be based on this example if it stood alone.

Strabo, from whom we gather nearly all we know regarding this temple, informs us, that at the foot of the statue of Apollo there was the figure of a mouse, and that both the statue and the mouse were works of Scopas of Paros. Σκόπα δ'ἐστὶν ἔργα τοῦ Θεμίου.[1]

On the extant silver tetradrachms, however, of Alexandria Troas, which bear dates from 137 to 235 of an era which may have commenced at the occupation of Alexandria by Lysimachus, B.C. 300, no mouse is figured, though there can be little or no doubt, from the peculiarity of the image of Apollo on these coins, that it is an imitation of the statue by Scopas. The figure is shown in profile, clothed in long transparent drapery, having a quiver at the shoulder, a patera in the right hand, and a bow and arrow in the left. On some copper coins of Alexandria and of Hamaxitos of later date, the same figure is seen, with the mouse at its feet.[2] There is some reason to think that Strabo had not himself seen the Sminthium, for he describes the temple as in Chrysa (ἐν τῇ Χρύσῃ), and adds that Chrysa was situated on a rocky height near the sea, a description which can answer only to the height which rises above Tuzla to the north, and which is separated from the Sminthium by the river Tuzla and the whole breadth of the plain Halesium.

[1] Strabo, xiii. p. 604.
[2] Mionnet, Suppl. v. p. 529-40, Nos. 70, 81. See also Urlichs, Skopas, pp. 111-113, who thinks that the figure of Apollo on these coins represents an archaic statue of the God and not the statue made by Scopas.

EXCAVATION OF THE TEMPLE OF APOLLO SMINTHEUS.

In pursuance of my agreement to excavate the site of the Temple of Apollo Smintheus and supply measured sketches of the remains, I left Smyrna for the Troad on August 5, 1866, for the purpose of presenting the firman to the Pasha of the Dardanelles, and for negotiating for the purchase of the ground on which the Temple stood.

Spiro, the Greek pilot who was with me at Teos, accompanied me as travelling servant. We landed at the island of Tenedos on the morning of the 6th. Here I learnt from the colonel in command of the castle that the Pasha was then at Luck, a town about three hours' ride from the landing-place on the opposite coast. We accordingly crossed the strait at once, and I rode on to Luck, where I found the Pasha on the point of leaving. He read the firman, expressing his willingness to afford me assistance in his power, and promised to send me a letter of authority (*buyuruldu*) if I would write him word when I intended to commence operations. I returned to the seashore the same evening, and at daybreak on 7th we left in a caïque for the Kulakli Scala, which was about three hours' sail to the south. We reached it in time to get to the village and summit of the hill which forms the northern boundary, and from the foot of this hill the ground slopes gently towards the centre ... the same day. I found the supposed site of the Temple in much the same state I left it four years before, except that there was more vegetation in the gardens than at the time of my former visit, which was late in autumn.

The wall which I then took to be part of the propylaea was still standing, but the slab of frieze which was near it had been broken up. This wall stands in the lowest part of a valley about half a mile wide and two miles long, which runs from north to south, opening into the plain of Tuzla at its northern extremity. On the other side it is bounded by high hills, for the most part barren. The village of Kulakli is built on the site and summit of the hill which forms the northern boundary, and from the foot of this hill the ground slopes gently towards the centre of the valley. This slope is entirely occupied by small gardens full of trees and watered by irrigation. In many of these gardens, and in the walls which enclosed them, I had remarked fragments of white marble, which appeared to have belonged to the Temple, but there was no mound of ruin, as at Teos, to indicate the exact site. In order to ascertain where the temple stood, I at first examined the neighbourhood of the mass of wall; but, finding no evidence that a large building had stood near it, I proceeded in the direction of the village, and examined the gardens and a road which intersected them. In one part of this road I perceived the edge of a squared stone, like a step, protruding above the general surface; and as, in the garden adjoining, there were several drums of columns and other stones lying about, I concluded that this must be the site of the Temple, and that the best plan would be to secure this garden for the commencement of future operations. An agreement in writing was concluded with the owner, and I paid down part of the price as earnest-money. Our business being concluded, we left on the 9th for Cape Baba, where there was a castle commanded by a captain to whom I had a letter, and who afforded me much assistance in future dealings with the inhabitants of Kulakli. We left our tent in his charge, and embarked in a caïque for Smyrna, which we reached in two days.

During the next fortnight I made preparations for returning to Kulakli. Through the kindness of the contractor for the Smyrna and Aidin Railway, Mr. Crampton, I obtained the loan of wheelbarrows, blocks, picks, and other implements required for the work; and on August 21 I started for Tenedos, taking with me Spiro and a Turkish carpenter. We landed the next morning, but were detained on the island for five days by rough weather. During our stay we were the guests of M. Tubuides, who was formerly British consular agent there, and who during our stay on the mainland was so kind as to afford us opportunities of communicating with Smyrna by means of the Austrian Lloyd's boats. Previous to leaving Smyrna I had written to the Pasha of the Dardanelles requesting him to forward the *buyuruldu* to Kulakli as he had promised. On August 30th we chartered a caïque to take the working implements to the walls at Kulakli, and by the evening of the same day we pitched our tents temporarily in a garden adjoining that which I had agreed to purchase. As no message had been received from the Pasha, we were compelled to limit our operations to cutting down the trees in the garden, pulling down walls, and perfecting our encampment. As up to the 7th of September there was no answer to my application to the Pasha, I sent a message to the sub-governor of the district, who resided at Aivadjik, a place nine hours' ride from our encampment, to inform him of the state of the case, and to request permission to dig, without which I should have met with opposition from the inhabitants. In answer to my application he came himself, bringing a letter from the clerk at the British vice-consulate at the Dardanelles, of which the following is a copy:—

"Dardanelles, Sept. 5, 1866.

"GENTLEMEN,

"It has been come to the knowledge of the authorities here that some gentlemen are trying to excavate in the district of Aivadjik and as this requires a permission or firman you are requested to show if you are provided with one.

"I have the honour to be, gentlemen,

"Yours respectfully,

"KURT FIGYEN,

"In Consul's absence."

Upon the receipt of this letter, I sent off a messenger to the Dardanelles, which is two days' journey from Keluldi, with a letter to Mr. Wrench, the Vice-Consul, who I heard had returned from Constantinople, begging him to speak to the Pasha and remind him of his promise. In four days' time I received a letter from Mr. Wrench, stating that he had at once obtained and forwarded the *boyurldi* containing permission to dig. No further obstacle being presented, I began work on September 13th by removing the soil which covered the stone step in the road, and in the course of a few hours I had the satisfaction of finding that in former part of the platform of the Temple. The next object was to ascertain in which direction the platform ran, and where it terminated. In order to do this, we carried one trench along the road, and another at right angles to it through the garden marked as that of Bairam on the Plan.[1] By the former were laid bare several steps, and beyond these we came upon a corner-stone of the pediment, showing that in all probability we were near the angle of the building. By the latter trench, which followed the line of the steps, and ran the whole length of the garden, we discovered a series of slabs of ragstone laid alternately with names of limestone at regular intervals, forming the foundation of the peristyle of the Temple. An architrave stone was dug up in the road, and its length was found to correspond exactly with the dimensions taken from centre to centre of the slabs of rag, showing that in all probability the columns stood upon these slabs. Thus it was evident that we had hit upon the true site of the Temple; but as the line of the steps ran due N.E. and S.W., contrary to the usual orientation, I was for some time doubtful whether we were working on the front or sides of the Temple. In a week's time, however, we had cleared all the foundations of the columns in the road and garden. These were too numerous to have belonged to one of the ends of the Temple. Therefore there was no longer any doubt that we were digging on the south-east side.

Having thus ascertained what we were about, I determined to excavate thoroughly Bairam's garden and the roadway to a distance of thirty feet from the edge of the steps, beyond which distance we could not reasonably expect to find stones, and to a depth equivalent to the depth of the pavement of the temenos below the ground level of the ground. This excavation occupied me until the 29th September. It was found that the steps had been removed, and that their foundations alone remained. But several interesting stones were found,—amongst them the corner-stone of the pediment, with a cymatium moulding and honeysuckle ornament upon it; outer and inner architrave stones—these being in the road, and in a better state of preservation than those in the gardens, which had suffered from lying in soil constantly wet by irrigation; three slabs of frieze in good style, but too much broken to be worth removal; a large stone, apparently a capital of one of the ante; drums of columns, and several wall-stones.

Thus far I had learnt little about the plan of the Temple; so, in order to ascertain what traces existed of it, I purchased the garden belonging to Kara Achmet, and a plot of Vakouf ground belonging to the mosque; and, as the soil was not deep here, in the course of a few days I had the satisfaction of laying bare the foundations of all the main walls of the Temple, though at the same time it was disappointing to find none of the upper courses in

position. The foundations were found to consist of large blocks of limestone laid transversely to the length of the building, and securely cramped to one another. The spaces between them were filled with small round stones, affording a foundation for the pavement of the Temple. At right angles to the main walls, other walls, 2 feet 7 inches thick, extended to the mass forming the substructure of the peristyle; the centres of these walls coincided with those of the slabs of ragstone upon which the columns stood. There were no pieces of marble that afforded any satisfactory dimension found in Kara Achmet's garden.

In the Vakouf plot we came upon slabs of rag and foundations of steps on the N.W. side; but as the ground fell away rapidly, whatever stones had fallen there had been removed probably for building purposes, with the exception of a piece of the frieze and some large blocks of rag.

Having ascertained the width of the Temple and its general plan, my next object was to obtain its length, and to see if any steps existed at the ends, though they did not at the sides of the building. For this purpose I obtained permission to dig in two gardens on the other side of the road, marked as Hussein's and Mollah Hassan's in the plan above referred to, and on October 9th I sent a party to work there. The three lowest courses of marble steps were found in situ in the middle of the front, but towards the W. the foundations of the steps had been removed, and the two lowest courses of limestone forming the general platform upon which the Temple stood were exposed to view. In Hussein's garden the excavations were carried to a distance of thirty feet beyond the line of the steps. The results were: stones of the cornice of cornice, a smaller cornice, and a stone of the laconaria, besides drums of columns and wall-stones. The exploration of this garden was completed by October 17.

In order to complete the circuit of the Temple we next dug up the gardens marked as Kazis and Mollah Mustapha in the plan. In the former the yield was excellent, consisting of a capital, pieces of architrave, a slab of frieze, and several pediment stones; in the latter, where there was not any depth of soil, an entire architrave stone and a few other stones of little importance were found. At this time I had two parties working, one here and the other in Mollah Hassan's garden. By the end of October, these diggings being exhausted, we attacked the three gardens which covered the N.E. end of the Temple, for the purpose of ascertaining if the arrangement at this end corresponded with that at the S.W. In Achmet Chianoff's plot we found the steps and some remains of the slabs of rag, besides several wall-stones, one base, and other stones. In Ibrahim's garden we uncovered the foundations of the N.E. portico; and in Kara Mustapha's the line of the lower platform was traced, so that I was enabled to obtain its exact length. Here was found a corner-stone of the pediment, and one or two construction stones; but the soil was shallow, and whatever stones had fallen here had probably been removed.

Having completed the circuit of the Temple, and carried the excavations to a distance of between 25 and 30 feet on every side,—except in one part of Mollah Mustapha's garden, where even the foundations were broken away,—and having thus obtained all the information that was to be gained about the Temple, on November 12th I commenced filling in these gardens, which I had arranged to leave level, and to build fence-walls. By November 22nd, all being completed, we left for Cape Baba and Mytilene; and, being detained at these places on account of quarantine at Smyrna, we did not reach that place until December 13th.

Remarks on the Style and Workmanship of the Temple, and on the Materials and Mode of its Construction.

From the bold character of the mouldings and general finish of the work it is evident that the Temple was

[1] This plan being of no general interest has not been engraved.

B

erected during a period of good but not of the finest art,—I should be inclined to place it between the dates of the temple of Athene at Priene and that of Artemis at Magnesia. The ovolo is long and pointed, and the mouldings generally are elliptical; the joints also are very neatly and smoothly worked. There is a certain difference observable between the workmanship of the capitals and between the sculpture of the frieze, showing that all were not executed by the same hand; but, on the whole, the style is of superior character, and there is much originality of treatment visible in both the capitals and bases.

Three descriptions of stone were employed in the construction:—

1st, *White Marble*, coarse in grain, with an occasional bluish tinge. This marble, which is less compact than Parian, was probably brought from the quarries near Cyzicus, in the Sea of Marmora. Unfortunately, on account of its soft nature, and the constant irrigation of the gardens in which the ruins lay, the surface of the marble was in many places very rotten, and the prominent mouldings, such as the flutes of the columns, are generally decayed and broken away.

All the external work was of marble.

2nd, *Ragstone* of a reddish tint, apparently obtained from the neighbouring mountains, in which there are rocks of this formation. This stone was in every case placed next to the marble, intervening between that and the

3rd, *Soft Limestone*, called by the Turks *cohendarsk*, which formed the chief mass of the foundations.

When newly quarried, this limestone, in colour and consistency, resembled compact earth well rammed down; but it hardened and became lighter in colour after exposure to the atmosphere.

The mode of construction was as follows:—

A large platform, composed of blocks of limestone, measuring generally about 7 ft. by 3 ft. by 2 ft. 6 in., was formed over the whole space to be occupied by the Temple. This was two courses in depth, and upon it were built the foundations of the walls and of the peristyle. These were also composed of similar blocks of limestone. Those for the walls were six feet long, of various width, and were three courses in height. Between the main walls and the mass which formed the foundation of the peristyle other walls, 2 ft. 7 in. in thickness and 14 ft. in length, were carried, one opposite the centre of each column. In some places these walls are four courses in height. Upon the limestone, and in every case between it and the outer casing of marble, were interposed slabs of ragstone. One stone of the course of rag remains in position upon the foundation of the cella wall, and in many cases these ragstones, upon which the marble steps were laid remain. The foundations for the columns consisted of two or more of these slabs of rag, measuring 7 ft. long by 5 ft. 4 in. by 1 ft. 6 in. These are to be seen on the S.E. of the Temple, and some of the second course at the N.E. end. From the great number of blocks of rag (some of which show a slope like that of the pediment) that were found in the gardens, and that are to be seen in the neighbouring walls, it would seem that they formed the core of the walls, the casing only being of marble. The marble steps at the S.W. end of the building are laid on rag, and securely cramped into it. The spaces intervening between the main walls of the cella and pronaos and between the side-walls were filled with round stones imbedded in earth, to form a solid foundation for the pavement. In one bay on the S.E. side these stones exist to the height of one foot above the level of the limestone foundation, and upon them is a layer of cohendarsk.

All the joints throughout are carefully made, and the whole has been securely fastened together with cramps and dowels run with lead.

Data for the Restoration of the Temple.

Plan. The existing foundations, when compared with the wall-zones, will give the plan of the cella and pronaos, but not with the same accuracy as if the lower course of marble had been in position.

As to the positions of the columns there can be no doubt, as the more solid foundations indicate their places, and the dimensions of the architrave, compared with the measured lengths of parts of the building, give the inter-columniations. No traces of the doorway or of their sites were found, nor were any fragments discovered of the architraves belonging to them.

Basement. The dimensions of the lower or general platform were obtained, and the relative positions of the steps belonging to it may be inferred from those still remaining *in situ* at the S.W. end. The form of the basement and the exact number of steps were obtained after the general plan of the Temple had been laid down, and the positions of the columns marked upon it (see Plan, Plate xxvi.) A small cornice, too large, however, to have formed part of the internal decoration, but not too large to belong to a podium, was dug up at the sides and front. This, no doubt, belonged to some part of the basement, and its position has yet to be defined.

The Order. With the exception of the height of the column, every part of the external order has been measured from the existing remains, so that its restoration is a very simple matter (see Plate xxix.) Of the *Base* five pieces were found, more or less imperfect; but they afforded the diameter and height, and they all appear to belong to the external order (see Plate xxx.) In no case was the lower torus perfect.

Of the *Column*, very few frusta were found that offered satisfactory dimensions, and none that belonged to the course immediately below the capital of the column. This upper drum is alone wanting to complete the height of the column.

Capital. Including the one found on Tuzla plain, five specimens of this number were found. The volute was in no case perfect, but enough remained to enable its form to be restored with very tolerable certainty.

The *Architrave* was in two stones. Several pieces of both inner and outer architrave were dug up, and two entire examples, both from the roadway, were also found. The upper surface of the inner architrave had shallow sinkings at regular intervals, apparently cut to receive wooden beams. Some of the pieces of the inner architrave had belonged to an inner angle of the peristyle.

Frieze. Six slabs of frieze were dug up, all corresponding in dimensions, the length of two of these being equivalent to the length of the architrave. The character of the sculpture on them varied, some of the figures being well, while others were indifferently, executed; but all were of better execution and proportion than those at Teos.[1]

On one of these slabs were represented two warriors armed with Argolic bucklers, and moving from left to right. Between them are the remains of a figure half rising from the ground, who raises his right hand towards the shield of the warrior on the left as if imploring mercy from his foe.

On another slab is a warrior armed with an Argolic buckler and cuirass advancing from the left and holding out in his left hand a tree or branch; on the right stand three small figures, draped, whom the warrior approaches.

On a third slab is a figure driving a chariot with two horses, who gallop to the right; behind stands a male figure.

---

[1] Sketches of these were sent home, but they are so much ruined that the interest they possess in their present state was not thought sufficient to justify the expense that would be incurred to engrave them.

All these figures are much mutilated, and only four have the remains of heads.

Cornice.—The cymatium, corona, and dentil stones were found in various places. The cymatium is ornamented with a fine honeysuckle ornament. The finest specimen of this ornamentation occurs on the corner-stone of the pediment (see Plate xxx. a).

Pediment.—Two of the corner-stones, together with several stones belonging to the tympanum, were dug up, so that the pitch of the pediment and its decoration can easily be ascertained.

Antæ.—Several stones, which appear to belong to the antæ, and which were apparently their capitals, were found on both sides of the Temple, but no stone belonging to their bases.

Cella Wall.—The lowest course of the cella wall has on it the base-mould. One example only of it was found. Several of the upper stones were turned up, and no doubt their respective positions can be ascertained by careful comparison.

In the cemetery of Turla, a village three miles from Kulakli, were several fragments of white marble with mouldings similar to that employed in the Temple (see Plate xxx. b, c). These were in good style, and would appear, from their superior character, to have belonged to the Temple, and to have been taken away to be used as gravestones. They possibly formed parts of the internal decoration, but their identification is difficult. Beyond these, no traces of the internal work were found.

It will be perceived from the above that all the data for the restoration of the external elevation, with the exception of the bases of antæ and the certain height of the column, have been recovered (see Plates xxvii. and xxviii.) This is almost as much as we obtained at Teos.

The stones wanting for a complete restoration of the entire building are:—

1. Base and capital of internal order.
2. The top stone of columns, and the drums of inner order.
3. Base of antæ.
4. Transverse beams. From the great length of the bearing, and the small size of the socket cut in the upper face of the architrave, it is probable that these, as at Teos, were of wood. If that be assumed, the transom stone would have to be placed in some other situation.
5. Angle capital of column. The angle capital was found at Teos, but it is hardly essential to a restoration, as its form may be conjectured by a comparison with other examples.
6. Marble covering of the roof. If the cross-beams were of wood, the roof would have been tiled. Many tiles were found on every side of the building, but none entire.
7. Mouldings of the interior. The mouldings of the interior, from their smaller size, seem generally to be the first to disappear. None were found either here or at Teos, and in most cases it would seem that the restorations of the internal ornamentation of Greek temples have been supplied by the imaginations of the restorers.

It will be seen that, though the Temple was a complete ruin, considerable information has been obtained as to its form and construction, and that it is interesting on account of its variation in plan and details from any other known specimen of an Ionic temple.

RICHARD POPPLEWELL PULLAN.

DESCRIPTION OF PLATES.

PLATE XXVI.

PLAN OF THE TEMPLE.

Though far from being entitled, from its dimensions, to rank among the first class of Grecian temples, the Sminthium is a fair average example of the medium class, in so far as size is concerned. It is rather smaller than the temple of Diana Leucophryne at Magnesia (ante, p. 15), but is considerably larger than the temples at Priené and Teos. It measures on the upper step 132 feet 8 inches by 68 feet 4 inches, but the value of these dimensions is considerably enhanced by the addition of a stylobate of ten steps, like that on which the temple at Ephesus was raised, which must have added very much to the architectural effect of the whole. Its greatest interest, however, lies in the fact that it is the most perfect specimen yet published of the pseudo-dipteral arrangement of Vitruvius (ante, p. 16).[1] As the pillars are less than 9 feet apart, from centre to centre, there could be no difficulty in finding epistylia of sufficient strength—which was the danger Vitruvius feared; but, as the distance between the columns and the walls of the cella is 10 feet, requiring lacunaria of nearly 20 feet in length, it is more than probable that the ceiling of the pteroma was wholly in wood, and this would be, in fact, the real defect of the pseudo-dipteral arrangement. In other respects its spaciousness and elegance have very much to recommend it, and go far towards compensating for the feebleness which, it is to be feared, is characteristic of the pseudo-dipteral arrangement.

The area at Priené is very similar in its arrangement to the Sminthium, and even a little longer, but, owing to the different arrangement of the peristyle, the whole area of the Sminthium is considerably in excess, that at Priené only measuring on the first step 7,816 feet, against 9,843 feet of the Sminthium. Whether the extended dimensions are or are not a gain, in an architectural sense, is difficult to decide. The Greeks, generally, seem to have preferred the more compact arrangement, and their decision on such a subject must be considered as final when expressed with sufficient distinctness.

PLATES XXVII. AND XXVIII.

ELEVATION OF THE FRONT AND FLANK.

The front and flank elevations of the Sminthium exhibit all the elegance that characterises the plan of the temple, but display the same comparative feebleness of design which, it is to be feared, is inherent in the pseudo-dipteral arrangement.

It is hardly in conformity with the principles of Greek architecture that the stylobate should consist of a simple pyramid of steps, as shown in the engraving. It is more probable that their length was broken up by pedestals at the angles, or by terrace-like masses on the flanks, as was,

more probably, the case at Ephesus, where a similar flight of ten steps existed (ante, p. 12). Nothing, however, was found in the excavations to explain how this was done—if done at all. It has, consequently, been considered safer to engrave them as perfectly plain, and give only their dimensions, 8 feet 7½ inches in height by 12 feet 3 inches in breadth, which seem to have been correctly ascertained.

In like manner, although it was ascertained from the discovery of the fragments, described by Mr. Pullan in his Report (ante, p. 46), that the frieze was adorned with reliefs, on the fronts at least, if not on the flanks also, these sculptures were so indistinct that the subject could not well be made out, and it has, therefore, been thought better to omit them in the engraving. In attempting, however, to realise the original design of the temple it must be borne in mind that a sculptured frieze did once exist. If it were now added and the stylobate broken up by pedestal and perpendicular masses, and adorned with statues, the design of the temple would lose much of that tameness with which, from its appearance on the plate, it may, perhaps, be only too justly reproached.

PLATE XXIX.

DETAILS OF THE ORDER.

The whole design of the order is of singular elegance, being sufficiently rich without being overloaded in any part, and every detail well designed, and appropriate. To modern eyes it may appear that it would have been better if the lower torus of the base had been bolder, as the whole seems hardly sufficient to support a column 10 diameters in height, which is, as nearly as could be ascertained, the proportion used. The capital is of usual dimensions and form, but between the volutes, on the space which is usually left as a plain sinking, a double spiral ornament of great elegance is introduced, which gives great richness to the whole, and is nearly if not quite unique. The acanthus, as introduced on the sides of the volutes, is also of great beauty, though its employment there would seem to indicate that the order was not of very great antiquity.

The entablature is of very elegant proportions, and such ornament as is applied to it is of great elegance, and distributed over the whole in a manner which is singularly appropriate.

PLATE XXX.

DETAILS.

Fig. A. The angle of the cymatium drawn to one-fifth the natural scale.

Fig. B. The ornament between the volutes of the capitals drawn to one-fifth the natural scale.

Fig. C. Section of the base of the column of the peristyle, drawn to one-fourth of the natural scale.

Figs. D. and E. Two fragments found at Tuzla drawn to half the actual size.

J. F.

[1] Vitruv., Proef. ed.—Dixta Minerva le symmetria Doric-que edibus ... deficit Minerva quod est Priene Doricus, Pallas; ... Hæc-quam de æde Diana Ionica quæ est Magnesia pseudo-diptera, et Liberi Patris Teo tetrastylos"

APPENDIX No. I.

MEMOIR ON THE PROPORTIONS OF THE IONIC TEMPLES OF PRIENE, TEOS, AND THE SMINTHEUM.

PRIENE.

The charm of Greek architecture has always been recognised as appealing to a sense of refined proportion, and its varied forms of expressive beauty, as graceful or majestic, elegant or imposing, to be largely dependent on appropriate proportional variations. Still further, a conviction has long been prevalent that the Greek architects in perfecting their designs were not content to rely upon an indefinite and general sense of proportion, but must have corrected them by the application of some system derived from rational scientific principles. Greek architecture has been called petrified music, and the metaphor is by no means incongruous. The human voice, no doubt, can be pitched harmoniously by a natural sense of delightful effect, and the eye may catch, and in like manner the hand may trace, very happy combinations of lines and magnitudes independently of a theory; the pleasurable and expressive effect in both cases is dependent on certain natural laws, but the full mastery of these is necessary if we are to hope for sustained and elaborate effects, for purity and finish, in either art. The eye is as spontaneously delighted by harmonious architecture as the ear by the harmonies educed from a musical instrument, but the instrument is only fitted to yield harmonious combinations in virtue of scientifically calculated dimensions and adjustment; and the architectural instrument, so to speak, is not exempt from the like obligations.

The treatises in which several Greek architects developed their systems are lost, and the rules which are given by Vitruvius do not justify themselves either by any natural propriety or by agreement with a single Greek building. Viollet le Duc, in his dictionary of architecture (Art. "Échelle"), expresses the difficulty of the problem though he does not venture to attempt its solution:—

"Nous ignorons le mécanisme de l'architecture grecque; nous ne pouvons que constater ses résultats sans avoir découvert, jusqu'à présent, ses formules. Nous reconnaissons bien qu'il existe un module, des tonalités différentes, des règles mathématiques, mais nous n'en possédons la clef, et Vitruve ne peut guère nous aider en ceci, car lui-même ne semble pas avoir été initié aux formules de l'architecture grecque des beaux temps, et ce qu'il dit au sujet des ordres n'est pas d'accord avec les exemples laissés par ses maîtres. Laissons donc ce problème à résoudre," &c.

Considerations of purpose and convenience, and regard to the nature of the materials to be employed, as wood or marble, furnish ever certain limits of proportion to the architect, but also with such wide margin of variation as not ever to decide dimensions absolutely; it is vain to expect from these conditions alone the evolution of exquisite expression and faultless beauty; these must have their origin in a mental conception, a birth of imagination; but if they are to be "turned to shape" and endowed with a "local habitation," the artist has need of all the assistance that can be derived from a theory drawn from the essential conditions and characteristics of his art.

The supreme beauty of the Parthenon has ever certified most absolutely that, whatever was the system by which its proportions were regulated, it must have had as true a scientific basis as that which governs the harmonious division of the monochord. This building, therefore, of which the measurements have been obtained by Mr. Penrose, with the utmost completeness and accuracy, represents the illustrations of a treatise of which the text is lost. The importance and advantage of the study of it from this point of view can scarcely be overestimated. The first condition for success in this study appears to be to realise by independent study of the problem of architectural proportion what are the structural terms a variable proportion between which would naturally have most effect upon architectural expression? When the value of a few such tests has been thoroughly certified, we have guidance as to the points at which to search for exact proportional adjustments in the great normal exemplar; the proof of the correctness of our original rigorous analysis is given by the first-fruits of its application being the acquisition of hints and instructions for perfecting still further our instrument of inquiry.

It is with the assistance of certified results from assiduous study of the chief monument of Athenian architecture that the present inquiry has been undertaken. It may be stated at once that the prosecution of this has brought home the conviction that in architecture, as in literature, it was at Athens that Greek genius attained its ultimate perfection. Neither in Sicily nor on the eastern coast of the Ægean do we find that the canons which the architects of the Parthenon discovered rather than invented are consistently recognised and strictly applied, and the crowning grace and last refinements of beautiful proportion are in consequence wanting.

There are indications however in the buildings which we are now concerned with of a much closer approximation to Athenian principles than can be credited to the Sicilians. It is not impossible that the Ionian architects may have had some elaborated system of their own, and have been prepared to vindicate it as an improvement. So far as any glimpse of such a system betray themselves, it has the

o

to the same, the intercolumn measures 1¼ diameters. The tidy uniformity of the equal spacing of plinths and intercolumns is thus at once relieved by the reduced diameter of the columns.

The interval from the plinths of the front columns to those of the ante was made equal to the plinths of the columns, and the central line of the flank wall of the cella ranges with the centre of the column in advance of it on the front.

The ante at either end centre laterally with the second columns on the flanks; and thus the wall has the extent of 17 plinths.

In these distributions we find the architect falling back upon a scheme such as is known as that of equal spaces, the pari quadrato of the Italians, which has great convenience in plotting, as it is by no means incompatible with a certain artistic effort in result. It has, however, no pretension to compare in richness of effect and scope of varied expression with the more profound and subtle, no doubt, more difficult instrument of the Athenian designers, who shunned, above all, repetitions of many dimensions reducible to identical aliquot parts.

The interior length assigned to the nave is nearly one-half the full length of the cella, namely, 8½ plinth breadths. 5·739 × 8½ = 48·87 to compare with 48·500 as measured. The actual length compared with the breadth gives us the ratio 7:11 with the trifling error of 0·15; trivial here, though we could not so account it in an Athenian structure.

This ratio may be held to fall into series with 3:11, which is that of the general ground plan. It is, however, a combination of numbers which does not seem to have found favour with the Athenian architects. The reduction of the length of the apartment by ⅓ of a foot would have given the very favourite proportion of 9:14.

$$9:14 :: 30·71 : 47·770.$$

Fifty Greek feet, measured from the further extremity of the nave, would fall pretty exactly in the middle of the broad threshold. This comparison is suggested by an apparent coincidence with an exact measurement in the Parthenon. From the practice of the best Athenian architects to derive our of their measurements from another proportionally, without reference to an equally divided foot-rule, we cannot expect to find many dimensions, even in a very large building, that fall coincidently with an exact number of feet or a leading and simple division of a foot. In the case of the Parthenon, of which we have the most complete measurement, it is much if an exact foot-rule measurement can be detected anywhere except as determining the hundred feet breadth of the platform. We might expect that at least a starting dimension importantly located would be found in every case; but, as it is uncertain whereabouts to seek it, so we shall scarcely be guided to the special received standard of particular localities and colonies.

Importance is given to the entrance to the nave, and expression of due support to the ponderous double valves which closed it by the thickness given to the cross wall. It exceeds the lower diameter of the column by one-eighth very exactly.

$$8:9 :: 4·23 : 4·750 \text{ (compare } 4·730 \text{ measured).}$$

The opening of the doorway itself has the noble dimensions of 15 feet, one-half the full breadth of the nave, the utmost that would admit of the valves folding back, if required, against the wall when the nave was thrown open.

The investigation of the proportions of the elevation of the temple of Priene appears at first unpromising from an unfortunate incompleteness of the monumental evidence. The appearance of the ruins before the excavations were commenced was such as to encourage the hope that valuable architectural members might be recovered from the ruined heap. The temple had manifestly been overthrown by an

earthquake, and what did not appear might be assumed to be buried, especially as, from the comparatively inaccessible site, the remains had not been largely resorted to for building materials. The most careful examination, however, after the site had been thoroughly cleared, failed to recover two most important elements of a restoration—the height of the column and that of the frieze. From the high finish of the structure it was naturally to be expected that the frieze would have been adorned with sculptures. Various slabs were found sculptured in relief, but not one that could be adopted as indicating the height of the frieze, even if there was a bare possibility that it might have belonged to it.

Numberless drums, again, of the thirty exterior columns, were found and measured, but all were in such confusion that it proved impossible to recompose them in a single instance in the order of original union; and, even more unfortunately, there was a uniform deficiency of drums that had belonged to the upper parts of the columns.

The student of the architecture of the temple of Priene is thus in the dilemma of a literary student who has to deal with a text which is partly corrupt and partly torn away. The recovery of a reasonable text is the condition of recovering the author's meaning; but the pursuit of it is onerous enough, even when the most has been made of hints from intelligible and undoubted context, and comparison of parallel passages from other works. The object in view, however, justifies the bestowal of considerable labour on the chance of a solution.

Study so effectual has been bestowed by Mr. Penrose on the question of the height of the column, and the satisfactory result gives 32·30 for this height without the plinth, the addition of the plinth raising it to 40·28.

As regards the frieze we have less satisfactory guidance. We can only take into account, in the first instance, the usual though not uniform practice of giving it a slightly lower height than the architrave; beyond this, to obtain a definite figure, we may assume conjecturally and under reserve that the relation of the two members at Priene may have been the same as in the temple at Teos. This would auth size architrave 3·330, frieze 2·880.

We have now, with this single moderate reservation, materials to determine the height of the front. The measurements are three;

Pediment	.	.	.	9·50
Cornice	.	.	.	2·08
Frieze	.	.	.	2·88
Architrave	.	.	.	3·53
Steps	.	.	.	3·13
Plinth	.	.	.	0·98
Base	.	.	.	1·77
Capital	.	.	.	1·57
Shaft	.	.	.	38·95
Estimated height of front	.	.	.	64·80

This total is only affected as an estimate—apart from a fractional uncertainty as to the frieze—by the height for the shaft of the column, which is taken from the result obtained by Mr. Penrose.

The breadth of the top step on the front is 81·00, and that of the intermediate 60·74, that of the lowest 60·60.

The approximation of the measure of height to that of the top step naturally suggests the possibility that the design made them equal; in this case the height of the shaft of the column would have to be reduced one foot, viz. to 38·10.

The objections to this are insurmountable, and the single alternative, if the architect is to be credited with having had regard to proportion here, is to assume that the symme-

tion of the pediment was regarded as a finish, which he did not take into account in deciding structural proportions. It is certain that an Athenian architect would either have made this particular agreement exact, or, if he thought it undesirable, would have effected some other exact and simple proportion.

It is open to question, however, whether the architect of this temple did not entertain some theory which induced him to vary from an exact equality of dimensions in execution. May not the excess of height, it may be asked, be an increment deliberately applied by him to counteract the reduction due to perspective. There can be no doubt that when the façade was regarded from any of the ordinary points of view, that is, from no considerable distance, it might have been made exactly as high as broad, but would not have told to the spectator as composed in a square. The height would be diminished perspectively disproportionately to the breadth. It may be thought that such a consideration would render all precise proportion in a large building nugatory. Rightly or wrongly the architect of the Parthenon did not think so, and took the greatest pains to make all such adjustments numerically exact as well as simple, having regard no doubt to general perspective effect in the first instance, as to what proportions he assigned.

The more minutely, however, we examine this building the more clear does it become that we are not dealing with an Athenian architect, but with one who had either principles of precise proportion of his own, which are very difficult to discover, or who trusted to a general sense of appropriateness and beauty for regulating his relative magnitudes, but did not in every case scrupulously subordinate to precise calculation upon the large and logical system of the architects of the Parthenon or the temple at Bassæ. No change which can reasonably be assumed in the estimated height of the building will accommodate at once a simple series of proportions to length and breadth, such as obtains with such marvellous minuteness in the Parthenon. The length of the bottom step is 127·276, which is more enough to the double of 64·80 (× 2 = 129·60), the measure of the height, to preclude the possibility of any other simple proportion having been aimed at. But even if the approximation were more exact, it would be anomalous for the height to be compared with the top step on the front, and on the flank with the bottom step.

In the Parthenon the height of the order, that is, of the entablature and column jointly, compares with the breadth of the top step in the ratio of 4 : 9 to the uttermost fraction of an inch. At Priene we have nothing better for an approximation than this, 5 : 1 : : 64 : 51·20, to compare with the measured 51·57, which is, indeed, unworthy to be spoken of as an approximation.

The contrast of the general proportions of this Ionic temple to the Doric Parthenon appears by the consideration that the fronts of both agree in height, within a few inches, while the breadth of the Parthenon exceeds 101 feet.

Height of temple of Priene 64·80, breadth 64·0
,, ,, Parthenon .. 65·16 ,, 101·341

The height of the column is the most important element in the determination of the height of the façade; but it is also the most important feature in itself, and one therefore to which others must be liable to be accommodated; the principle on which its proportions are regulated may therefore be considered independently, though it may have been originally determined by a comparison.

If it had been held of importance in this instance, as in the Athenian, to make the full height of the front agree by precise proportion with its breadth, it might seem that the full height distributable among all the members of the order being given, the height of the column must be

limited. But, on the other hand, the previous decision as to the height that the column must be allowed was more likely to limit the proportion available for the height of the façade to its breadth.

In passing now to the consideration of what is technically called the order, we are bound by the analogy and authority of the great Athenian examples to search first for the principle on which the total height was proportionately distributed between the proper vertical member, the column, and the joint height of the horizontal members, the epistylia in the fullest sense and the hypostylia. The predominant contrast lies here, and here in consequence the function of definite proportion to conciliate contrasted elements is peculiarly in request. It was a principle of the Athenian architects to decide this distribution by a ratio of the simplest class, that is a superparticular ratio, or one having a difference between its terms of unity; as 1 : 2, 2 : 3, 3 : 4, &c.

In the present instance the contrast is regulated by a proportion taken between the shaft of the column and the complement of the height; that is to say, the architect, having in view to give the utmost enhancement to verticality in his design, chose to throw the capital and base of the column into the complement, on the justifying grounds that in these sub-members taken individually horizontality predominates. The result of the comparison gives the favourable ratio of 3 vertical : 2 horizontal.

3 : 2 : : 38·90 shaft : 25·97 complement
38·96 shaft

64·93 to compare with 64·80 as estimated.

The difference is not more than may be corrected by addition to estimate of frieze. By the stratagem of throwing the base and capital into the horizontal term of the comparison some other important symmetries are conciliated. In Athenian architecture it is always a study to bring the height of the column into a double relation; first by such a proportion to the complementary horizontals as we have just identified, and then to an extent measured laterally between centres or margins of columns. In the present instance the height of the shaft gives a dimension which comprises on the plan four diameters of columns and the three intercolumns to compare with height of shaft, 38·96.

The shafts of the four central columns are therefore contained in a square.

The column is completed to its full height by the addition of heights of plinth, base, and capital, 4·20 to the shaft 38·96 = 43·280, and it will be observed that the joint heights thus added are nearly one-tenth of the full height.

But the column proper, that is, exclusive of the plinth, is 42·60 in height or exactly ten diameters.

The diminution of the shaft of the column, or the difference between the upper and lower diameters, is one-seventh.

7 : 6 : : 4·20 Lower diameter : 3·62 (compare 3·60 measured upper diameter.)

This completed column now accommodates one of the proportions upon which the Athenian architects by their practice at least laid most stress; it compares as the vertical member of the front with the joint height of the horizontal members in a superparticular ratio, in which it represents the superior term, namely, 1 : 2.

64·8 ÷ 3 = 21·60 (compare measured complement 21·52)
43·20 (compare full column as taken 43·28)

64·80

There is, however, a certain anomaly in taking, as we have done, the simple shaft of the column as the typical vertical member in two comparisons, and thus deserting it in a third, and the most important perhaps of all. It is more correct, therefore, to test the relation of horizontal and vertical members by comparing the shaft and complement of height, that is to say, by regarding capital and base as allowably grouped with the horizontal members in accordance with the predominant direction of their lines and dimensions.

We obtain by this comparison the equally appropriate ratio 2 : 3.

64·80 ÷ 5 = 12·96 × 2 = 25·92 Cf. complement 25·81
× 3 = 38·88 Cf. shaft . . 38·99

$$\overline{64·80} \qquad \overline{64·80}$$

The dimension assigned to the three steps, the proper basement, exceeds that of the base and plinth of the column which it immediately supports by one-fourth.

4 : 5 :: 2·75 : 3·437 to compare with 3·430 measured.

We have now out of our full height of 64·80 feet disposed of 40·717, viz.:

Full column . . . . . 43·980 ⎱
Steps . . . . . 7·437 ⎰ = 64·80
Leaving for pediment and entablature 18·083

In the distribution of this the superiority is given to the pediment to the extent of one fifth above the entablature;

18·083 ÷ 11 = 1·643 × 5 = 8·215 for entablature measured 8·29
„   6 = 9·868 for pediment measured 9·86.

The entablature is slightly affected by the element of the estimate of the frieze.

The correctness of the estimate of this is however confirmed by its agreement with the joint height of the capital and base;

Capital 1·57
Base   1·77

3·34 ; Cf. height of architrave 3·35.

The cornice is very nearly one-fourth of the height available for the entablature 8·29 ÷ 4 = 2·072; Cf. 2·08 measured.

The remainder is divisible between frieze and architrave, of which members it was most important to regulate the latter by a rational proportion.

The height of the capital is to that of the base previously as 8 : 9.

8 : 9 :: 1·57 : 1·77 as measured.

TEOS.

The temple of Teos like that of Priene has six columns in front and eleven on flank. Excluding some additional steps on the east front it has five steps instead of three only; the lowest step compares in breadth with that at Priene as 72·33 : 69·6; and in length as 120·9 : 127·27.

The larger plan however contracts as we recend, and the hexastyle front at Teos, measured to the plinths at the angles, compares as 58·50 only with 64·0 at Priene.

	Teos.	Priene.
Height of front .	48·265	64·80
Diameter of column .	3·080	4·200
Height of column .	31·205	43·28
Intercolumn .	7·030	7·335

It will be observed that there is a remarkable coincidence in the absolute dimensions of the intercolumns; but a great contrast in effect is produced by the relatively more open spacing at Teos, the much smaller proportion which the diameter of the column bears to the intercolumn. At Priene the intercolumn measures one and three-quarter diameters, whereas at Teos it is as much as two and one-sixth. 13 : 6 :: 7·33 : 3·08 (Cf. 3·080 lower diameter).

Otherwise stated, the intercolumn compares with the joint diameters of the columns on either side as 13 : 12.

At Priene the predominance in this latter comparison is given to the solid above the void as 16 : 14.

It is manifest that the most critical proportion in the design of a hexastyle Ionic temple was that which regulated the width of the inter-columnar space relatively to the diameter of the column.

The size adopted for the column is conditional on the magnitude proposed for the work and required for its purpose, and the openness of the spacing adopted affects most importantly the expression of the completed design.

The determination therefore of absolute diameter and relative spacing decides a certain limit for the breadth of the stylobate and even more importantly the axial lines of the cella walls which range with the second columns from the angles.

The temple at Teos has six columns on the fronts, and eleven on flanks, counting the angle columns both ways; it has therefore five columniations on the fronts, and ten on the flanks; and the centres of the four angle columns are thus as at Priene on the angles of a double square.

The columns have Attic bases on plinths, and the plinths are not brought close up to the edge of the step as at Priene, but a clear margin is left as much as 1·28, which harmonizes with the general effect of open spacing.

The same may be said of the greater breadth of the steps at Teos and their wider spread.

There is a variation here on the two fronts; at the west the basement consists of five steps and a sixth as offset, and these are returned along the flanks; but at the east or principal front there is a further descent accommodated by an extension of six steps additional.

The steps on flank spread so far that their width together with that of the ambulatory up to the cella wall is just equal to half the width of the cella from out to out.

The cella therefore is just half the full width of the plan of the temple on the step common to all the sides.

The same dimension measures the corresponding extents on both fronts, from the edge of the same step to the face of the ante of the cella; a uniformity that on Attic lines, always on the look out for enrichment of his boundaries by variation, would certainly have avoided.

The lowest step of the west front and flanks proves to have a proportion of 4 : 7, nearly enough to leave no doubt that it was intended; 7 : 4 : : 125·975 : 72·000(Cf. 72·332 measured).

A less moderate addition of equal margins to the original double square would have given the proportion of low numbers 5 : 9, but the next such proportion reached by further extension is 4 : 7, and it has the advantage of effecting the equal distribution of breadth between cella and surroundings which has already been noticed.

The proportion adopted for plinths to interplinths is 7 : 8, and their absolute dimensions 5·0 : 5·70 are obtainable by the apportionment of the columniation by this ratio into eight-fifteenths and seven-fifteenths.

The columniation or space from centre to centre of column is 10·79; the diameter of the column is 3·08, which leaves 7·32 for the inter-column; these dimensions are in the ratio of 6 : 13.

13 : 6 : : 7·32 : 3·08.

Consequently the proportion between the void intercolumns and the joint solid of the adjacent columns is 13 : 12.

The ante and cross walls of the cella range exactly with the axes of columns on the flanks. The pronaos is deeper than at Priene, where it was square on plan; at Teos it has the proportion of 6 : 7.

7 : 6 : : 32·650 : 24·155 (Cf. 28·031 measured).

The ante has the proportion 13 : 18 very exactly ;

18 : 13 : : 38·80 : 28·00 (Cf. 28·03 measured).

There is no step from ambulatory to pronaos, and only a single step from pronaos to naos.

The height of the column taken, as at Priene, exclusively of the plinth, is nine diameters:

3·38 × 9 = 30·42, to compare with 30·155 measured.

The nearest approach to a lateral symmetry for the columniation is obtained by comparing the full height of the column with the extent from the centre of one column to the nearer edge of the lower diameter of a fourth; that is to say, to the sum of three columniations less one semidiameter:

10·70 × 3 = 32·10 − 1·09 = 31·41 (Cf. 31·295 measured height of column).

This result cannot be considered as likely to tell in effect. The breadth of the four columns in front of the mass taken on the plinths would compare with the height of the columns by the ratio 7 : 6 exactly:

7 : 6 :: 37·10 : 31·80.

The addition of another diameter to the height of the column would have given a symmetry from centre to centre.

The diminution of the column is nearly in the ratio of 6 : 5:

6 : 5 :: 3·38 (lower diam.) : 2·817 (Cf. 2·860 measured upper).

On Plate XXIII. we have the dimensions inserted of 4·040 for the upper series of five steps, including the cymatium; but by reference to Plate XXIV. it will be seen that one more step, or rather an offset, should be included in the set of those which are continued all round the temple; the addition completes to the proper height of the general steps 4·863. Consequently, the comparison of full column to complement is thus established:

Height of pediment, 6·75
„ entablature, 6·18 } 17·793 : column 31·295
„ six steps, 4·863 }

These dimensions only have the proportion of 4 : 7, with a difference that is too serious to be accepted, and we miss the superparticular ratio which is normal for this comparison of vertical and horizontal.

But if, following the analogy of the other Ionic examples, we take the shaft of the column alone as one term, and add the joint heights of capital and base to the horizontal, we obtain for complement

4·023 capital and base.
17·793 pediment, entablature, and steps.

Full complement, 21·816 : shaft of column, 27·242.

This gives very exactly the required superparticular ratio, viz. 4 : 5:

5 : 4 :: 27·242 : 21·809 (Cf. 21·816 measured).

The height of the front taken as 48·265, independently of the offset, compares with the breadth of lowest step, approximately only in ratio, 2 : 3:

2 : 3 :: 48·265 : 72·397 (Cf. 72·532 measured).

Again the full height of the east front including the additional steps compares with the breadth of the lowest step in the proportion of 3 : 4:

1 : 3 :: 72·532 : 51·250 (Cf. 51·055 measured).

These are not such coincidences as we are accustomed to expect and to be gratified with in the proportions of the Parthenon; and yet they are sufficiently near to certify that they do not occur by accident. The difficulty of obtaining precise measurements of structures in such a lamentable state of ruin as this temple may be answerable for some of the differences that perplex us; but something may probably have been due to original laxity in execution. A rigorous exaction of minutest finish, whether in large works of art or small, is only the characteristic of the most refined epochs of art and the very centres of cultured taste. When Plato in the Laws (x.) is arguing for the universal

supervision of Providence, he refers with confidence to the analogy of the scrupulous care which artificers bestowed equally upon small stones and large; but Plato found his examples on the Athenian acropolis.

The sum of heights of capital and base compare with the lower diameter of the column in the proportion of 6 : 5.

6 : 6 :: 3·380 : 4·056 (Cf. 4·033 measured).

And to the further distribution advantage is assigned to the base above the capital in the proportion of 11 to 10.

11 : 10 :: 2·115 base : 1·920 (Cf. 1·918 capital).

After deduction of the height of the five steps made equal to the joint height of the capital and base 4·040 : 4·033, a dimension is left which, divided between pediment and entablature in the proportion of 10 : 9. At Priene the height of the pediment has the larger advantage of the entablature by the proportion of 11 : 10.

The architrave has the same proportion to the frieze as the base of the column to the capital.

11 : 10 :: 2·380 : 2·163 (Cf. frieze measured 2·160).

The wide spread of the steps and also the comparatively low entablature harmonize with the very open spacing of the columns; but the effect of the unusually depressed pediment does not appear equally satisfactory; it is difficult to think that it was not relieved by acroterial ornaments of considerable importance; but no remains of such were found.

THE SMINTHEUM.

The temple of Apollo Smintheus is contrasted with those at Priene and Teos, both in proportions and plan. It is octostyle instead of hexastyle, it has an even number of columns on the flank, it is pseudo-dipteral, that is to say, the ante of the cella range with the third columns from the angle front and flank, and a broad ambulatory is obtained by the omission of any second rows of columns in line with the second columns from the angles. There is thus the further difference that the temple is elevated upon a basement so much higher and more widely spreading than that at Priene, and which, unlike the high basement at Teos, is continued all round.

The diameters and heights of the columns of the three temples compare thus:

Teos 3·380   Smintheum 3·870   Priene 4·230
„ 31·295   „ 38·70   „ 42·30

The columns at Teos are the most openly spaced, and those of the Smintheum the most closely. The absolute dimensions on the top steps are:

Teos . . . . 61·118 : 114·864
Priene . . . . 64·00 : 121·079
Smintheum . . . 74·080 : 132·670

The bases of the columns, unlike those of the other two temples, are without plinths.

The columniation of the Smintheum is equal front and flank, and the oblong of its plan taken upon the line of centres of columns would thereby, according to their number, have the proportion of 7 : 13.

The extended dimensions of the proper stylobate yield a simpler ratio, but only approximately:

9 : 5 : : 132·67 : 73·705 to compare with 73·05 measured.

The oblong of the lowest step ratio only approximates to the proportion 8 : 5:

8 : 5 :: 157·09 : 98·18 to compare with 98·50 measured.

This proportion, to be exact, would require a breadth of steps, diminished front and flank by 0·65, or 156·21 : 97·65.

The lower diameter of the column is proportioned to the intercolumn; as 2 : 3 approximately:

2 : 3 :: 3·870 : 5·805 to compare with 5·895 measured intercolumn.

The axis of the cella range with the third columns from the angles front and flank. By the extension which is given to the steps on plan the dimension from the edge of the lower step to the cella wall on flank and the anta in front just equals the breadth of the cella.

This wide spreading basement has a manifest harmony with the exceptional breadth of the ambulatory.

The ambulatory has the same breadth at either end of the temple as on the flanks, a uniformity which is quite alien to the taste and practice of the Athenians, who as already noticed were eager for opportunities of harmonious, however slight, variations.

The cross-wall with the doorway of the naos is so placed as to allow an exact square for the plan of the pronaos clear of the line of the columns in antis.

The transverse wall of the posticum, of which the axis ranges accurately with the centres of columns of the peristyle, limits a mass which has very accurately the proportion on plan of 5 : 3 :

5 : 3 :: 1141 : 20·66 (compare measured breadth, 20·655).

The columns have a diminution of one-seventh:

7 : 6 :: 3·870 (lower diameter) : 3·317 (3·294 measured upper diameter).

The height of the column is exactly ten lower diameters : 38·700.

These proportions agree with the design of the Priene columns, of which the height is 42·00, and the diminution, therefore, slightly less quick.

The height of the base is obtained by the proportion of 2 : 3 to the lower diameter of the column :

3 : 2 :: 3·87 (lower diameter) : 2·58 (height of base as measured).

From this height of base the height of the capital is thus obtained by the proportion 7 : 6 :

7 : 6 :: 2·58 : 2·211 (measured height of capital, 2·225).

The height of the column being obtained we are again directed by knowledge of Athenian practice to inquire for a coincidence either of the full height of the column or of the shaft with some marked limits of their lateral distribution.

The full height of the column gives no satisfactory or plausible terms of comparison between centres or margins, or between a centre of one column and a margin of another; the height of the shaft, however, very exactly measures the extent of three columniations and one diameter of a column on the plan: thus the extent of the four bases which are in front of the cella, with their intervals, is equal to the height of the shaft of the column.

At Priene a like extent on plan measures the height of the complete column; in the still more openly spaced temple at Teos this lateral dimension is less than but proportionate to the height of the column.

When the diameters, spacing, and height of the columns are determined, certain general limits are obtained by the usage of the style for the dimensions of the epistylia, the entablature, and the pediment.

The entablature may approach but not exceed a height which is double the lower diameter of the column, and in consequence will be less than the measurements of a columniation; the pediment considerably exceeds the entablature in height.

At Teos indeed this excess is but trifling, and to such lowness of the pediment together with the unusual poverty of its mouldings, is due to the inferiority of general effect in the façade.

Again the breadth given to the basement enforced a certain number of steps and thus settled a certain limit of their joint height.

In result these approximations were reduced to proportion by giving the basement the superiority to the entablature in the proportion of 7 : 6, and the pediment above the entablature in the proportion of 8 : 2 (= 9 : 6).

7 : 6 :: 8·620 basement : 7·300 (measured entablature 7·104). This is the proportion of the lower to the upper diameter of the column and also of the height of the base to that of the capital.

3 : 2 :: 11·100 pediment : 7·40 entablature as measured. This is the proportion of the intercolumn to the lower diameter of the column and also of the lower diameter to the height of the base.

9 : 8 :: 2·680 architrave : 2·568 (frieze measured 2·560).

3 : 2 :: 2·889 „ : 1·926 (compare cornice measured 1·955).

The return of the cymatium of one the flank entablature makes it nearly equal to the height of the steps.

If we were dealing with a structure by fictions it would be a question how far the joint dimension to be distributed between pediment, entablature, and basement, was not dependent on consideration of what dimension would complete an eligible proportion of height of the front to its breadth, and then of complementary height to height of the columns.

In the present instance the full height of the front, the sum of the dimensions reviewed, is 65·825, and this compares with the breadth of the top step very satisfactorily.

9 : 8 :: 73·08 top step : 65·85 (65·824 measured height). But it compares in a still simpler proportion with the wide bottom step:

4 : 3 :: 98·50 breadth of bottom step : 73·90 (74·08 measured).

With the length of the topmost step it is nearest to the proportion 1 : 2.

2 : 1 :: 132·67 length of bottom step : 66·335 (cf. 63·824).

The full height of the front as measured is divisible between the column 38·700 and complement of height 27·124.

10 : 7 :: 38·700 : 27·09 for complement.

The superiority is here duly given to the vertical member and the result is sufficiently accurate numerically, but the Athenian architect preferred to regulate this comparison by one of the simpler proportions which have only a difference of unity between their terms; 10 : 8 = 5 : 4, or 7 : 8, &c.

W. WATKISS LLOYD.

APPENDIX No. II.

ON THE ENTASIS AND HEIGHT OF THE COLUMN OF THE TEMPLE AT PRIENÈ.

The height of the columns of the temple of Athenè can only be obtained indirectly from the measurements of the fallen drums. The fragments of no particular column could be put together with certainty, and Mr. Pullan was only able to find about one-fourth of the original number, and of these the stones from the lower parts of the column formed by far the largest proportion.

The plan which first presents itself in an attempt to recover the original height is to superimpose one upon another drums which have like dimensions in their top and bottom beds respectively, but this is soon discovered to give no satisfactory solution. Mr. Pullan found the flutes generally so much worn that he was obliged to take the measurements within the flutes, and an additional element of uncertainty is thus introduced, for no column has ever so perfect a contour within the flutes as it has upon their edges. It thus happens, as will be seen from the subjoined measurements of the drums, that many of these stones, whilst they have like measurements on their top and bottom beds, vary very much in length, so that it is possible by this process to arrive at results quite discordant one from another. The measurements of the drums, however, seem nevertheless capable of affording a very close and reliable result when fully discussed, and I have from them deduced a value in which I have great confidence. Mr. Pullan fortunately measured all the drums which were calculable, and for the lower three-quarters of the column, at least, they are sufficiently numerous to enable us to get rid of the accidental errors, both of workmanship and of measurement, and to determine a very close approximation to the original character of the entasis, and from it to deduce the heights.

If the shaft of a column were to diminish without entasis, and therefore should be truly conical, it would only be necessary to measure a sufficient number of drums and no could obtain the rate of diminution, and as the upper and lower diameters are supposed to be known, and in fact in this case are known, the height would at once follow. But in the case of Prienè, as of all good examples of ancient Greek architecture, the contour of the shaft is a curved line, and the question thus becomes more complicated; nevertheless it may be completely capable of solution if there be a sufficient number of drums of all diameters. This is nearly the case at Prienè but not quite, as those near the top of the column are rather scanty, but I consider that this deficiency may be got over in a satisfactory manner and a close determination arrived at.

To understand the method about to be followed, let it be first assumed that the shape of the entasis is known as well as the amount of diminution and the vertical height.

Divide the given horizontal quantity, that is to say the whole difference between the upper and lower semi-dia-

meters, into a number of equal parts, say not less than eight, and plot these distances down along a base line. Then draw perpendicular lines through the points so obtained to meet the curved outline of the column and join the intersections. These last straight lines will then form part of a polygonal figure, the height of which will by construction be that of the column exactly, and each of the sides will show the rate of diminution of the column between the corresponding horizontal diameters plotted down upon the base line. That is, would show the angle of inclination of the shaft of the column between these points.

The same result would follow if the horizontal subdivisions were not exactly equal; but to make a good approximation to the shape of the column they must be sufficiently numerous and properly distributed.

Conversely if the angles of inclination corresponding to given horizontal differences were given or determined we could draw the proposed polygonal figure, and should thus discover both the form of the entasis and the height of the column, and it is on this method that the following calculation is founded. For convenience, the differences of diameter instead of semi-diameter are used in what follows, but that does not affect the result:

TABLE I.

	Diameters within the flutes		Height of Drum		Diameters within the flutes		Height of Drum
	Top	Bottom			Top	Bottom	
1	·5¾	·2¾	9·72	13	·57	·59	9·65
2	·52	·55	1·25	24	·55	·57	1·00
3	·53	·55	1·90	25	·55	·53	9·50
4	·54	·55	9·52	26	·55	·58	9·84
5	·75	·58	9·75	27	·55	·62	3·74
6	·29	·31	1·95	28	·55	·58	9·95
7	·49	·55	9·71	29	·55	·59	9·97
8	·50	·55	9·95	30	·55	·60	9·75
9	·41	·57	9·95	31	·56	·59	9·95
10	·47	·55	9·58	34	·57	·59	9·54
11	·55	·58	9·63	33	·57	·62	9·77
12	·55	·59	9·58	34	·57	·54	9·74
13	·55	·55	9·54	35	·57	·61	9·95
14	·56	·59	3·16	36	·58	·65	9·95
15	·58	·59	9·53	37	·58	·60	9·54
16	·58	·51	9·71	38	·58	·59	1·75
17	·58	·55	9·52	39	·59	·61	9·61
18	·50	·50	1·93	40	·58	·63	9·71
19	·19	·52	9·45	41	·59	·50	9·95
20	·59	·57	9·53	42	·59	·64	9·90
21	·53	·58	9·04	43	·60	·63	1·99
22	·53	·58	3·94	44	·61	·71	9·95

TABLE I.—continued.

	Diameters within the flutes		Height of drum.		Diameters within the flutes		Height of drum.
	Top.	Bottom.			Top.	Bottom.	
	feet.	feet.	feet.		feet.	feet.	feet.
45	·66	·61	4·60	71	3·69	3·75	3·59
46	·67	·63	3·19	72	·69	·66	1·28
47	·67	·65	3·13	73	·70	·73	1·38
48	·63	·66	3·45	74	·70	·73	3·43
49	·63	·66	2·80	75	·70	·74	3·06
50	·64	·69	2·61	76	·70	·73	3·81
51	·64	·68	3·45	77	·71	·73	1·71
52	·61	·70	4·25	78	·71	·78	2·98
53	·60	·60	3·50	79	·71	·73	2·95
54	·60	·62	1·81	80	·71	·70	4·28
55	·66	·67	1·90	81	·72	·63	3·03
56	·65	·69	3·03	82	·73	·76	3·12
57	·66	·72	1·60	83	·73	·75	2·46
58	·67	·69	2·44	84	·73	·75	3·11
59	·67	·70	2·81	85	·73	·75	2·68
60	·67	·71	3·45	86	·73	·76	3·50
61	·69	·71	2·82	87	·74	·77	3·01
62	·68	·72	3·08	88	·74	·73	3·95
63	·68	·71	3·33	89	·71	·78	3·08
64	·68	·73	3·82	90	·71	·80	3·68
65	·69	·75	4·15	91	·74	·76	3·47
66	·69	·76	4·57	92	·74	·78	1·90
67	·69	·76	1·91	93	·76	·80	1·18
68	·69	·70	2·64	94	·75	·78	2·33
69	·69	·75	3·50	95	·76	·79	3·63
70	·69	·72	3·74	96	·77	·81	4·50

TABLE II.

MEASUREMENTS OF BOTTOM DRUMS WITHIN THE FLUTES TAKEN AT THE TOP OF EACH.

	Diameter, feet.	Length, feet.
1.	3·820	4·700
2.	3·820	4·370
3.	3·810	4·350
4.	3·810	3·870
5.	3·800	3·840
6.	3·800	3·820
7.	3·790	4·360
8.	3·790	4·820
9.	3·790	4·150
10.	3·790	4·100
11.	3·790	3·100
12.	3·785	4·280
13.	3·780	4·700
14.	3·780	4·100
15.	3·770	4·350
16.	3·760	4·180
17.	3·760	4·100
18.	3·755	3·875
19.	3·730	4·070

Mean diameter derived from the first fifteen, 3·795.
Full diameter above the apophysis being 4·280.
Derived diameter above the apophysis within flutes 3·890.

Mean length of drum, 4·200, of which the apophysis occupies 0·65. It is assumed that the last four may belong to the inner order.

TABLE III.

MEASUREMENTS OF UPPER DRUMS WITHIN THE FLUTES AT THE BOTTOM OF EACH DRUM.

Diameter, feet.	Length, feet.
3·350	1·980
3·335	2·180
3·330	1·980
3·300	2·680
3·323	2·145
3·300	2·480
3·285	2·120
3·280	2·800

Mean diameter derived from the first six, 3·328.
Full diameter below apophyge being 3·600.
The derived diameter within the flutes below the apophyge, 3·257.
The mean length of the drum is 2·26s, of which the apophyge occupies 0·70.
It is assumed that the last two drums may have belonged to the inner order.

From the measurements above recorded I form eight groups, namely:

TABLE IV.

A. Number of drums in group.	B. Observed extreme diameters of the drums.	C. Rate of diminution per unit of height.	D. Number of drums of each kind assumed.	E. Range in feet of the horizontal diminution.
1 Ten	feet. 3·77 to 3·74	··	··	·
2 Twenty-two	3·74 to 3·70	··	··	·
3 Thirty-one	3·70 to 3·65	··	··	·
4 Twenty-five	3·65 to 3·60	··	··	·
5 Eighteen	3·60 to 3·45	··	··	·
6 Eleven	3·45 to 3·40	··	··	·
7 Eight	3·40 to 3·35	··	··	·
8 Three	3·35 to 3·25	··	··	·

In computing the column C of this table, the numerator and denominator are respectively proportional to the sum of the differences of diameter, divided by the sum of the lengths; and in forming column D weights are assigned to the different drums in each group proportional to their lengths, and placed as if acting at the mean diameter of each drum, and the centre of gravity of the whole is then taken for the general mean point.

Column E, which is derived from Column D, merely shows the horizontal range of each group, and extends from the top of the lowest drum, which contains the apophysis of the base, to the bottom of the uppermost drum, which contains the apophyge of the capital.

A small correction, however, has to be applied to the column C of the table, as explained below, which leaves the rates of diminution at the different points as follows:

TABLE V.

		C.	Horizontal range.
Group 1	·	··	·0420
" 2	·	··	·0370
" 3	·	··	·0650
" 4	·	··	·0890
" 5	·	··	·0665
" 6	·	··	·0790
" 7	·	··	·0715
" 8	·	··	·0245

This readjustment of the rates of diminution is based on the following considerations. Firstly, the rates of diminution derived from the longer drums are entitled to some preference over the shorter, if only that the probable errors of measurement are smaller in proportion to the derived diminution. In order to arrive at this adjustment I have calculated a table on the supposition that the drums are entitled to preference in proportion to their lengths, and obtain those ratios for their denominators, namely:

In group 1 for 80·01 . . . . 97·3
    ,, 2 ,, 79·20 . . . . 81·3
    ,, 3 ,, 82·00 . . . . 77·0
    ,, 4 ,, 74·20 . . . . 73·4
    ,, 5 ,, 72·60 . . . . 68·8
    ,, 6 ,, 65·91 . . . . 64·6
    ,, 7 ,, 83·95 . . . . 53·7

As however the errors of measurement are probably not more than one-fourth of the inequalities of workmanship in the interior of the flutes, I have taken one-fourth of the range between the two tables, and the denominators of the fractions in Column C, Table IV. then become

TABLE VI.

1	. .	91·50	5	.	71·65
2	. .	79·72	6	.	65·15
3	. .	80·75	7	.	53·90
4	. .	73·55			

But there is also another correction required. The groups of drums must necessarily admit some from the practice and position, which were less uniform than those of the peristyle in the proportion of 1 to 7½, and they were also rather smaller in diameter, namely, the lower full diameter was 4·160 instead of 4·250. This diminution would exclude these drums from groups 1 and 2, but in the third and subsequent groups they would be liable to enter, and must be eliminated, on the consideration that for every 7½ drums in group 3 one may have belonged to the interior order having a rate of diminution proper to group 1 or 2; that in group 4 there is an element of the same nature, having the diminution proper to group 3, and so on. This problem admits of easy solution, and the result is the sort given in Table V.

We may now build up the column in this manner, namely:

The base . . . . . . 1·770
The mean height of lowest drum . 1·209
·0420 × 91·50 . . . . 3·843
·0070 × 79·72 . . . . 2·050
·0050 × 80·10 . . . . 5·206
·0830 × 72·91 . . . . 6·053
·0065 × 71·35 . . . . 4·745
·0790 × 64·26 . . . . 5·077
·0715 × 53·40 . . . . 3·818
·0245 × 30·17 . . . . 0·831
The mean height of the topmost drum 2·205
The capital . . . . . 1·570
                                    42·342

As however the last two groups are not based on a sufficient number of drums to be implicitly received, it will be

desirable to test the result above given by another method. Let us therefore consider the first six groups only as established, and then proceed as follows. Reckoning the shaft proper from the top of the apophysis, the diameter within the flutes is 3·826 and the height of the mean lower drum above this point is 3·649, and therefore to the No. 5 point of Table IV. 20·356, with a diminution of ·329 (namely, 3·826 − 3·497), but the total diminution to the bottom of the apophyge of the capital is ·369. The object will now be to draw a straight line from the bottom of the shaft which shall represent the chord of the entasis, which we have already traced for about two-thirds of its extent. This done, I assume that the column had an entasis proportional to that of the Erechtheum. Less than this very delicate curvature would have been unlikely, whilst it would not have been much more pronounced without strong disagreement not only with the pieces derived from the sixth, seventh, and eighth groups, but also with the general sequence of the curvature given by the first five points, which can hardly be questioned.

The horizontal distance between the chord and the figure we have traced through the first five groups which would be required to produce an entasis proportional to that of the Erechtheum is 0·053; let this be added to the ·329 already stated as the diminution up to the No. 5 point of Table IV., making it ·382, and the following simple proportion will obtain:

total height of shaft $\frac{20·356}{·369} = \frac{·382}{}$ from which results the quantity 35·24; then the total column will be—

Base . . . . . . 1·77
Apophysis . . . . . ·65
Shaft . . . . . . 35·24
Apophyge . . . . . ·70
Capital . . . . . 1·57
                        42·05

The two methods are, to a great degree, independent of each other, and combine to point out that the height must have been very nearly if not exactly ten diameters, which would be 42·33, and I consider that the limits of error do not admit the possibility of any other definite proportion of diameters, or of halves or quarters of diameters.

There is a peculiarity to be noticed in the form of the entasis as thus determined, namely, that the principal amount of curvature is found towards the top of the shaft, whereas in the Attic examples it occurs either near the base or towards the middle. If, as has been done in The Principles of Athenian Architecture, an hyperbola were chosen to represent the curvature of this entasis, its vertex would be above the capital. In all other ancient examples known to me, this maximum curvature occurs either below the shaft, as in the case of the Parthenon, or in some part of the shaft itself.

F. C. PENROSE.

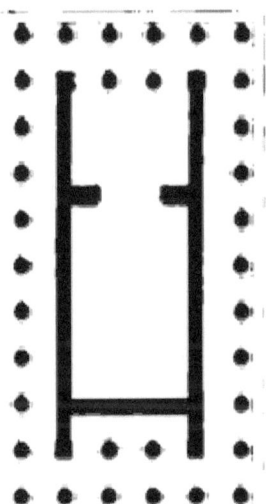

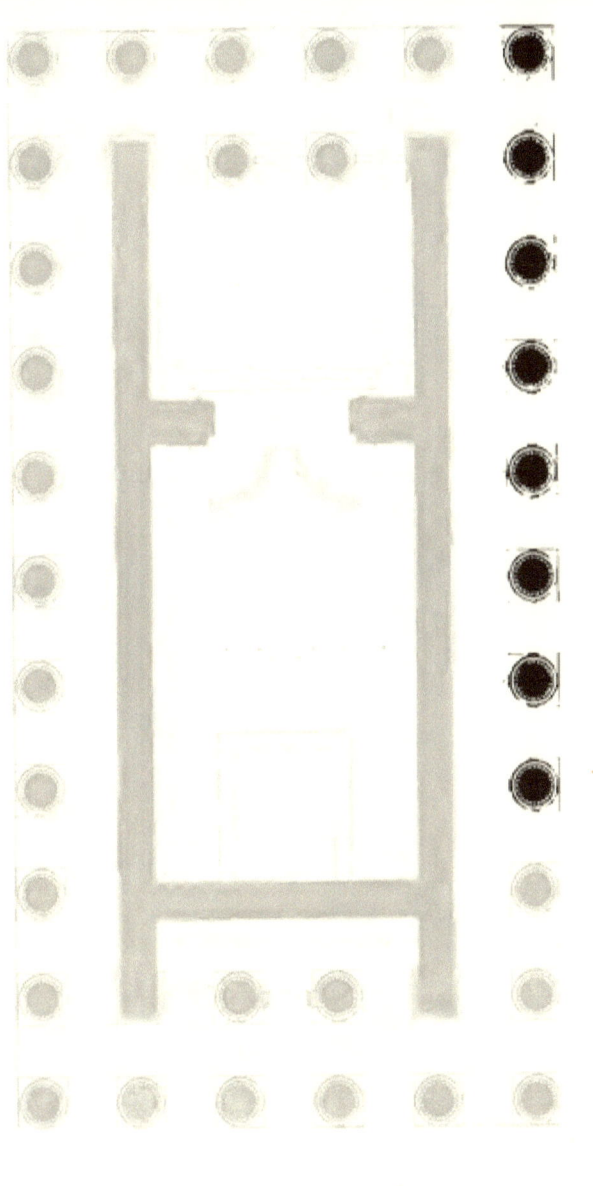

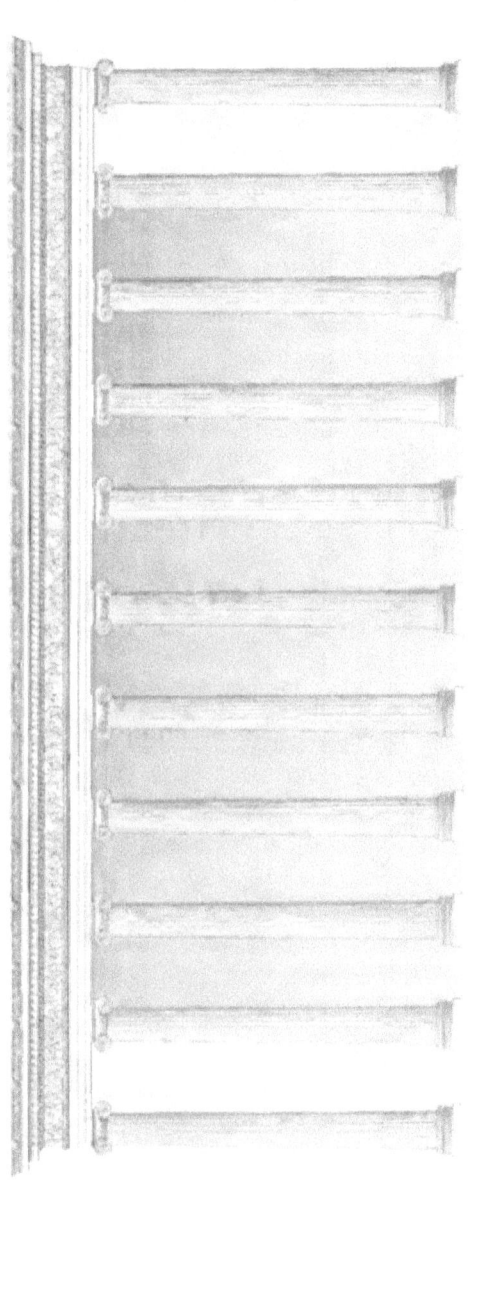

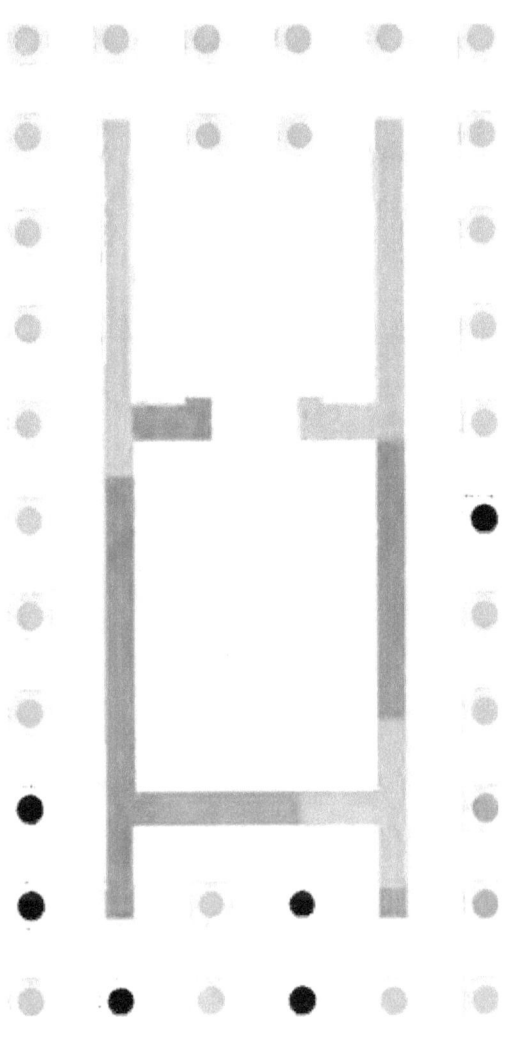

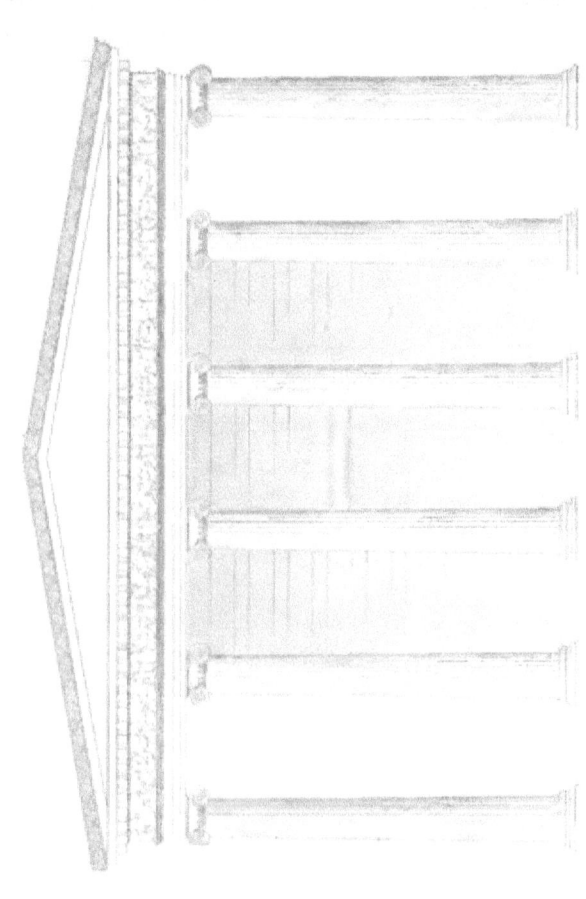

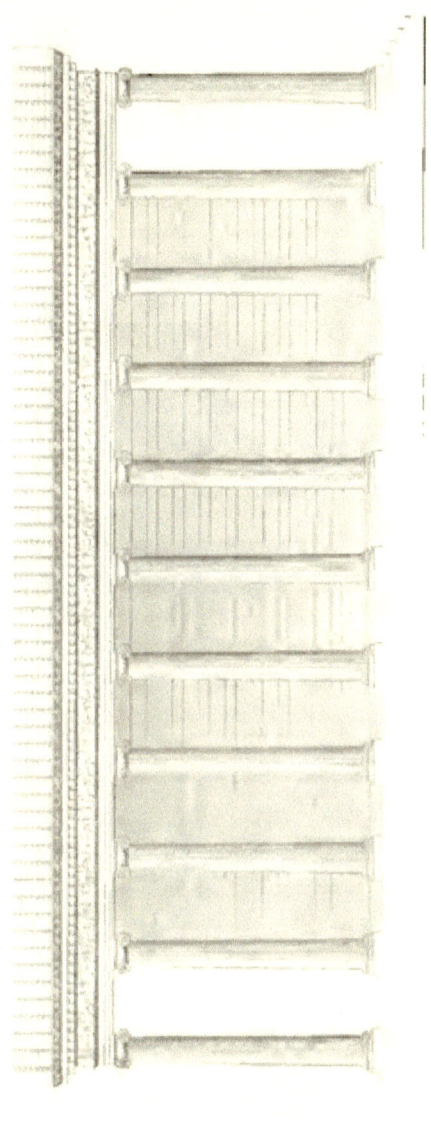

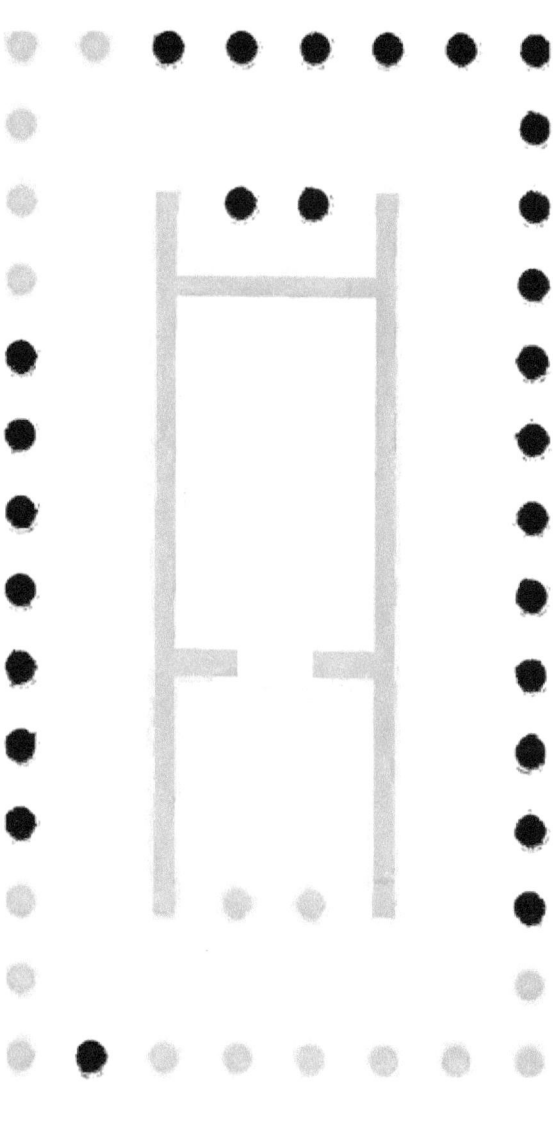

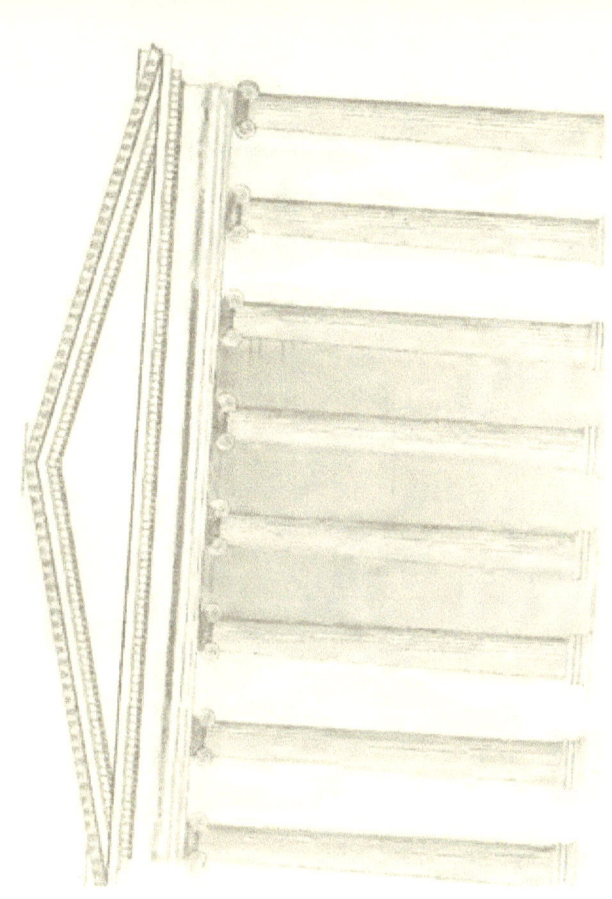

www.ingramcontent.com/pod-product-compliance
Lightning Source LLC
Chambersburg PA
CBHW020757020726
47495CB00008B/2481